~ Gaea ~

The Faery Door

by T. Powell

Shanti Publishing Company
Berkeley
2016

First Edition

ISBN 978-0-9882569-3-4

Shanti Rare Book and Publishing Co.
PO Box 2515
El Cerrito, CA 94530
www.shantipubs.us

For Rio
- T.A.M.M.S.M.

And for Ellena and for the twins
-wherever they may be

Chapters

Foreword

Recently, here in San Francisco, a series of events did unfold which awakened people to the presence of the magic all around us. The news media reported some facts and speculations, but just as a legend may bear more meaning and even more truth than the facts upon which it is based, this fictional story is arranged and told so as to more clearly reveal the actual meaning of the appearance of the little door in Golden Gate Park - much more than have all the news reports, rumors, and official statements. It is actually a keenly honest confession of the magic of which the world is entirely composed.

While I had originally intended it to be a child's story, the tale seemed to grow on its own, blooming like a tree with some large and strange words coming to roost among its limbs, so I have included a glossary of the more esoteric ones - such as the word "esoteric" - and am issuing it as a tale for children of all ages.

I've used a more traditional spelling of "faery", to differentiate somewhat from what the word "fairy" usually conveys today - a stock image of diminutive human figures with the wings of butterflies, which is not necessarily wrong, but quite limiting. Being spirit, they may assume whatever form may best suit their mood, use, or desire. And while on occasion, throughout centuries of recorded history, the faery folk have been observed mimicking human appearance in some fashion, many of the faeries of Earth have never even seen a human. Most of them are wild, meaning they hold not to our laws or morals, just as most of Earth is still uncivilized, and inhabited by all those wild beings who greatly outnumber us. The fae alone outnumber us too.

There are a couple of plural forms of the word "faery": "faeries", which is used to indicate a number of individuals; and "fae", which may be used to refer to a group of them collectively. As a proper noun, "Faery" is used to refer to them as a class or species, or to their whole magical realm.

My method of interpreting the Faery speech found woven through this tale is based on a principle learned by experience. That is, if one is truly to see or hear a thing, one must look and listen not just with the ears and eyes, but with his or her entire being, completely willing to encounter whatever may be.

And it is my hope that anyone who follows this trail of words along the vistas and wonders through which it leads, may by trail's end be inspired enough to listen for and to hear the Faery speech for themselves.

- T. Powell

The Faery Door

I. Magic

It was an evening no more miraculous than any other...

The sea bowed low in prayer, spreading wide the shimmering of her robe, as the sky bloomed like a rose.

The dunes gave up their push to cross over the Great Highway and settled along its edge, letting the breeze softly sculpt their rippled slopes, while a lone pelican soared idly down the long mirror of shore. The cypress trees held wide their lush limbs for a last embrace of light from the West.

A downy, tuft-haired little babe sitting up in her wooden crib gazed on the colors dancing in through the window. She never questioned the obvious fact that these little gleams with their hearts of light were alive; neither did she believe that this brilliant moment might ever one day fade from her memory, though a few of those lucent little flames for some reason seemed to be carrying a shade of sorrow in the midst of their dance of the blossoming stars.

Dusk settled and rolled the trails into shadow, and the sparrows huddled under the warm robes of spruce. The oaks and elms were softly growling to one another, while the grasses whispered themselves to sleep, and twilight revealed their dreams.

The stout-hearted redwoods stood their heights under

a nightfall of diamonds, across whose eternities Orion the hunter followed the star-haloed stag.

It was an evening as magic as any other; and as usual, hardly anyone noticed.

Orion

II. Glimmerings

A pruned garden of little lights, each one a glowing eye in the night, the city kept watch for her wayfaring soul; but over the green grandeur of Golden Gate Park, and its woods and meadows and lakes, starlight was lord. It softly illuminated the trees and slumbering leaves of grass, as well as the roofs of the de Young Museum, the Academy of Sciences, and the boathouse on Stow Lake, and its little firefly glows played in the waters.

A loose huddle of people walked out through the landscape of the De Young, and along the twilit sidewalk by the Japanese Tea Garden where the fallen cherry blossoms had been layered on the trails, and where the tiny daisies had been left opened this night - each one tuned to follow its own star so as to be the more radiant for when the morning fog would come drifting in from the sea.

Peering down the dark way, the silhouetted people trod almost blindly past the glorious bloom, toward their vehicle parked against the curb, two of them staring fixedly at the luminous faces of the electronic devices they clutched in their hands as they followed along. As with most folks, the world surrounded them with beauty they rarely saw, offering adventure they never seized.

A faery, crouched amongst the fallen petals like a sapphire glimmer of moon on this moonless night, watched an owl swoop quietly over their preoccupied heads and doubted that these folks had even noticed much in the museum.

Another little faery appeared like a crimson moth to dance across the little gleam of moonlight, teasing and inviting it to play.

But the little blue glimmer was worried for the people of this planet, who more and more seemed unable to simply look around and see their own sunwashed world and its wild soul of green.

The faeries spoke like whispering doves as the daisies listened, and the two decided that they would call a Faery Ring to be held on the next full moon to decide what might be done to help awaken these human folks.

Inspired with hope, the blue faery unfurled her clear wings, and they sailed on the breeze over to the island on Stow Lake where a chorus of moss-green frogs, arranged around its shores of stone, were chanting along with the rise and fall of the night surf.

And meanwhile, on the other side of the Twin Peaks, over in the Mission District, a child whose dark brown hair was a soft tangle, and whose eyes were deep pools of soul, sat watching the turning wheel of sky. He had just closed the astronomy book his Nana had given him, and now the stars were glimmering in many hues and flashing down as if to say, *"You are right - there is more to the world. Keep looking!"*

The constellations sailed across the black depths, like his dad out at sea. He opened the book again to the pages reserved for notes, and taking up his pencil he wrote these verses, reciting aloud to the night:

> *"Some may call me adventurous*
> *for I ride the wind and sail*
> *out into the wine-dark sea -*
> *the stars all gazing back at me*
> *and letting fall their veils.*
>
> *They call me adventurous*
> *though we share the quest and lot -*
> *aboard this earth, in twilit seas*
> *of terrible immensity -*
> *Some see it; some do not."*

III. The Faery Ring

A pearl white beam of the full moon shone down through the looming redwoods and into a woven ring of holly and mistletoe which lay upon the forest floor. No one had come jogging through the little clearing since nightfall, but the moon shaft glittered with swaying strands of dust motes swimming lazily within it like silver schools of tiny fish. Gathered around the holly and mistletoe wreath were a score of softly luminous fae from around the park lands.

One of them stood near the Faery ring clutching a strange fiddle carved of knobby cypress wood. Her dark and gleaming eyes reflected the glittering stars and the vast reaches through which they wandered.

Now seeing that the wood was clear (of humans), she bowed toward the moonlit circle and played the cypress fiddle.

The tune began like a star being born to rise in budding flame and dawning glory, resounding deep in the bones of the earth, rocking the roots and embracing the whole forest but not consuming it in its warm green fire.

The enraptured fae of the gathering gracefully danced around the moon-held wreath with its berries red and white, some of them riding the currents of song and hovering 'round one another in various hues of the wild blooms; and they sang together in tones of waters running over mossy stones, and of mellow gusts through the reeds.

They sang the rose dawn of history, of distant constellations and great celestial migrations -

and the stars above were fascinated, and listened from their thrones hung high in the unbroken expanse.

They sang of Faery and the bringing of life to the scattered turning worlds -

and the mossy redwoods hearkened, nodding in remembrance of ancient generations of forest, many lifetimes past.

They sang the earth mother and her luminous horizons.

And the blue faery whose wings were clear as water told of the human spirit, how bright it had shone in and around the people, until the falling of the dark age in which they shut their doors to the voices of the night. And their fear of darkness covered them until even the stars appeared strange and distant, and all the creatures of the twilight seemed hostile to them. And what had once been lovely and bright was now dull and weary - for ever since had most of humanity been ruled by the unwieldy burden of fear.

And she and the others there sang of the vow they of Faery had taken after the fall of the people - to remain unseen as are the four winds who cast no shadow.

A dark faery sang of how some of them had come

across the great sea and over the wide land to this coast where only a few gentle people were dwelling until recently when more and more of those folk from the other side came over too, crowding out the native ones, and obliging the fae even here to remain almost perpetually within their veils of mist and sorcery.

Rather would they have remained free to shine in the open field and evening skies, but they would not trust those who were fear's slaves.

And the little choir of hawk feathered fae chorused the clear winds who, unafraid of the days or the nights, pull the white sails and lift the fair wings; they throw wide the seeds and dance among the green things growing.

They sang all this with but the voices of brook and breeze, ultimately asking with the final phrase of the fiddler's tune, *"These people drowning in their own darkness - how may we show them the door back to the light of the world?"*

And just then the dust motes in the moon shaft stilled their dance, and held a shape these fae well knew - that which resembled the leafy, budding boughs of one of the elm trees in the park.

The faeries' eyes reflected for a moment the luminous dust as they saw the design, and then they whisked up the sprigs of mistletoe and holly to weave little crowns for one another, and were then swiftly away with the dream they had just witnessed, now aglow in their hearts and soon to enflame the world.

The dust motes then began to drift back up toward the frost white moon whence they had come, and by the time they had risen beyond the tree tops, all that was left of the dance in the redwoods was a new ring of moon-pale mushrooms who awoke in the soft blue light just before the dawn.

There weren't even any visible footprints, and not so much as a speck of litter, although sometimes after a Faery Ring one might find a small, vibrant feather fallen, or a tiny fiddle string.

THRUSH

IV. Something New

It was a morning similar to other mornings:

Wild geese rose from the lake, heralding the dawn in harsh trumpets.

The dreamy mist gave way to the rising sun and drifted back toward the sea, trailing a silver cape over her footpaths of dew.

The ghost lady who wanders Stow Lake at night shrank away from the dawn and went back to rest within her night-scented cypress tree.

The finches yawned and shook out their little wings, while the thrushes were already foraging in the soft meadow and filling the air with streams of water-clear melody.

Golden warmth arrived and spread like a low flame. Blooms of fragrant lupine, wild onion, and blackberry opened up for the bees to find; and the feathery yarrow - which sprouts up wherever the light of Mercury touches down with winged sandals. Sprinklers cast shimmering rainbows over field and hedge, and each tree unfurled its limbs and rejoiced in the holy embrace of light.

It was a morning as miraculous as any other, but this one arrived to find something that none of her other sisters had ever seen.

V. Close Encounter

In the grove of elms near the de Young Museum, a little boy with thoughtful brown eyes and a tousled shock of earth brown hair stood watching a gopher pushing up fresh dirt and peeking out of his hole back up at the boy who seemed gentle enough. Then the morning breeze stirred the leaves and the boy looked up in time to see a starling alight upon a high limb and break into rapture, singing of the bright sky and sunwashed earth. His plumes were dazzling in the sunlight and his song filled the air with invisible wings, declaring to other birds in the area, *"Here I am! Me - the song of the fiery blue... I am here!"*

As the music stirred him, the boy began to hear along with it what sounded like a harmony of ethereal strings, which gently tugged his attention down to the base of another elm nearby. And what he saw there was something out of a dream.

There hung a small, finely crafted wooden door. It was about six inches tall and shaped to fit neatly into a little archway at the foot of the trunk. Its finish was smooth, but patterned like the bark of the tree, so that even with the hinges of bronze, it would have been quite camouflaged were it not for the light glowing behind it now like an eclipsed star. It was closed and a soft music of unearthly beautiful voices was sounding from behind it. An old, storm-polished bud stuck out to serve as a little knob.

About fifty yards away sitting near the great fountain

where the panther and serpent were frozen in battle, the boy's mother was studying a row of stones they had collected that morning. Her black and grey hair just reached her collar, and her dark eyes were intent as she sketched in her field journal. The boy had been in the process of creating a little labyrinth there on the ground with her stones when she had got annoyed and told him to go play in the grove. There were no other people around but them.

He didn't mind going to play alone. Away from other people, he often got the feeling that there was much more to the world. While he loved his friends (most of whom were books and the dead poets who had written them), and while never would he have wished for a different family - although his had broken in two - he had always felt most at home among the grass and trees and birds and stars, the steadfast rocks, and the wild waves, and the wordless song of the sky. His name was Rio, which in Spanish means "river".

Slowly he walked over to the little door and crouched down beside it in the shade. There was a magic here that he could not explain, but which also seemed familiar to him somehow, like some lost memory which had for years shown up only in his dreamscapes. He knocked on the little door and waited a few seconds.

There was no answer except a feeling that someone really wanted to come out of there and play. He knew his mom would want to decide whether or not this was something they should even be messing with, but he had already decided he was not going anywhere without seeing what lay behind it. He reached down, grabbed the little knob and pulled the door open.

Light washed over him like a tide, embracing him in a glow that was, rather than the brazen sun, more like moon and starlight. Little gleams of colors flying 'round him dazzled his dark eyes. He heard bright, melodic laughter of many voices and he felt he was on the threshold of another world.

He lost sense of time and place, but when the light retreated back into the door he was a little surprised, a little relieved, and also a little sad to notice he was still in the grove that morning, although everything - every leaf, cloud, and stone - now appeared to him as new creations, fresh from the artist's hand.

The little door stood open and the light and music became soft again like the warm embers left over from a once blazing fire. Then as it closed and blended back in with the tree, Rio thought that now someone would have to know it was there to find it.

He saw his mom through the trees, still making notes about rock classifications or something. Slightly dazed, he walked over to her.

Mom looked up to see the boy standing in front of her still looking a little confused but bright eyed, gazing around as if he had just been told a very funny story but was still trying to figure out the punch line.

"What's up, Rio?" she asked him.
The answer dawned in the boy's eyes. He looked at his mom and said, "Faeries!"

Before taking her back to see the faeries' door, he made her promise not to tell anyone, and then he dug into his backpack and opened the book he had been reading - The Human Comedy, by William Saroyan - and taking his mom's pencil in hand, wrote inside the front cover, the poem that was now blooming in his heart:

> *"I*
> *believe*
> *in nothing*
> *but miracles."*

Rio

VI. Words

From the Sierra to the sea, the wide, fallen land lay open to the endless sky, awaiting the touch of light and rain.

The clouds intertwined into stanzas of grace, and let their holy waters fall over the fertile earth and her dreaming seeds.

And they burst forth in warm blooms - horizons of fiery petals; echoes of the humming, distant suns.

So too are the words on this page but magic seeds, blooming only with the touch of light and a shower of grace.

A California Spring, Albert Bierstadt, 1875

VII. Secrets

Rio was out on the covered back porch of their old blue and magenta Victorian house in the Mission neighborhood, watching the rain as it dripped from eaves draped with grape vines, and into the redwood flower boxes placed around the edges of the deck; and listening as it washed over the willows in the yard which sloped down to the creek, where the little frogs were chirping merrily.

His mom had hurried them home after seeing the virga hanging from the northern clouds which were coming their way. She liked the idea of rain and hydration for the environment, but not since she was a young girl splashing through the sun glossed rains of the great valley had she enjoyed the touch of it too.

Kneeling inside by the stone hearth, an array of somewhat rare rock samples standing in line on its mantle, Mom was thinking about Rio's finding of the curious little door in the elm tree, and wondering whom they ought to tell about it. She knew Rio wasn't too keen about trusting other adults than her, not since his dad had left them, but this was perhaps an important and valuable discovery.

The burning wood had been slightly rain sprinkled and damp, and was now especially smoky and fragrant. She rose and walked back through the kitchen to the screen door of the back porch, and said through the fine mesh, "Rio, come inside by the fire."

"I'm alright, Mom," he said. "I'm not getting wet."
The smoky sky swept its touch over the trees and grass, the rooftops and the hills in the distance. Seeing Heaven and Earth come so close together, he began to breathe in time with the falling waves of rain.

Mom stepped out cautiously. She thought it rude to continue speaking through a closed door. Rio focused on the blank page of his book and wrote down some new verse:

> *"They called this day ugly*
> > *but it was only the rain*
> > *unleashed and bounding home:*
> *Its somber meteors*
> > *in free, ardent fall -*
>
> *The grey winds graced*
> > *with descending, loft seas,*
> *And beauty the dark dunes*
> > *of storm will bring...*
> *Not veiling it at all."*

The tide of inspiration was in flood this day, and he closed his eyes to see more clearly his visions.

Mom caressed her folded arms. "I think we should tell someone from the University about your find," she said.

Rio was quiet.

"I'm just not sure which department to go to first," she continued.

Rio sighed. "None of them," he said. "They don't have a 'Faeryology' department, do they?"

"No, but we're talking about an uncategorized life form," said Mom. "Maybe the Biology Department would be interested."

"I don't think they're cellular, Mom," Rio said with less patience than usual. "The biologists wouldn't know what to do except refer me to the Psych department for evaluation."

"Rio, I think I know a little more about this than you."

"I wish you did know a little more," Rio said.

"Hey Dude," said Mom. "I'm just trying to help."

He looked up at her, into the brown eyes that always clearly showed what her heart held. "I know you are," he said more kindly. "I'm just not sure people are ready for this."

"But the Faery folk seem to think we are," she said. "They wouldn't have announced themselves if they thought we couldn't handle it."

"They lit it up for me alone," said Rio, "and I showed it to you because you promised not to tell anyone else."

"But if they know anything about people, they know how gossipy most of us are," Mom said. "They must be counting on you spreading the word." The willows seemed to nod in agreement. "Just tell one more person," she said earnestly, "without imposing secrecy upon them, and I promise I'll let you be."

Rio watched the strawberry leaves in the redwood boxes getting bombarded but shaking off the drops of water.

"Look... I'm letting this be your decision," she began, trying to wear an air of graceful importance, "but... TELL PEOPLE!"

"Alright," said Rio, still gazing down. "I'll tell Morgan, but that's it."

"Morgan?!" said Mom.

Rio smiled.

"The Morgan who took a vow of silence!" she said. "Is that the Morgan you mean?"

"That's the only Morgan I know," said the boy.
"And what is that going to accomplish?" asked Mom.

"Ending this argument?" Rio suggested hopefully.

Mom's eyes flashed and narrowed, but although Rio had expected wrath, what he saw was pride. Sometimes she loved it when he won.

"This isn't over!" she said dramatically, both of them knowing it was obviously over.

Walking around the deck, she looked over the first budding blooms of strawberries, then gathered some mint, fresh grape leaves, and some Miner's Lettuce, and brought them with her back inside to make a salad of early Spring.

Rio picked up his football from the little wooden shelf against the house. The willow trees - called the "Whispering Ones" by the Ohlone Indians who not so long ago had lived around here - seemed to be weeping in the gentle rain, and Rio thought he could cheer them up by kicking his football into them. He also wanted an excuse to catch a little rain himself. He walked to the edge of the deck and punted the ball across the yard and into the rustling limbs. But instead of flinging it back like they often did, they somewhat peevishly dropped it. Rio heard the frogs cease their merry song, and knew that they had chucked it into the creek. He ran through the silver shower - down the steps, across the wet grass, and down through the dripping willow trees to the stony creekside - and picked up the ball from where it lay among the rushes. A Blue Heron who had been stealthily wading upstream on its frog hunt, stood eyeing him with a mixture of fear and outrage. The boy had ruined its plans for lunch.

Walking back up the slope, Rio paused among the willows. It was here that Dad had told him about the divorce, that he would be moving out to live aboard his sailboat, the Golden Bough, and also that they wouldn't be seeing each other for a few months because although he was but a novice sailor, Dad had decided to sail around the Pacific Ocean on his own.

That was already a few months ago, and the last Rio had heard, the Golden Bough was down near the Juan Fernandez Islands, off the coast of Chile.

Rio didn't understand why his dad couldn't have put some of that fiery imagination and questing energy into saving his family.

The willows wept with him as he wondered if it was raining out at sea.

Moving on across the grassy yard, he spotted a solitary weed maturing into a wildflower, blushing deeply to catch the boy's eye.

He knew that his mom would probably weed it out, but right now - as the sun gracefully parted the crowds of white angels to shine upon this little scarlet paintbrush - she danced fearlessly with the rhythm of the world, an eternal flame.

Running up the back steps and onto the covered porch, he dropped the ball and picked up his book where he had laid it, to put down in words this new inspiration, but then he heard his name being shouted: "RIO!!" - loudly enough to rattle the screen door.

And Mom stated, quite loudly still, that Rio was soaking wet.

Rio said that actually he considered himself at this time to be only damp, or perhaps one could say that he was merely moist.

Mom told Rio that he had to go and take a warm shower before he would be allowed to have lunch, which she had just finished preparing. The look in her eye told him not to try arguing that taking a shower would make him more wet. He did offer the defense that his football had rolled down to the creek, but this he said as he was already taking off his sneakers to go in and comply with her demands. Slightly dripping over the desk in his room, he took a moment to open his book again and write:

> "Her blush is warm Aurora's glow
> in subtle, ever changing hue;
> More subtle still, to see her grow,
> unfolding into form anew;
>
> To stir in sky-lashed breezes, and
> the light of golden sunfire's kiss;
> Her wild aura teases in
> a buzzing honeybee to this.
>
> And so she springs to flaming bloom,
> casts wide her seed; in ashes falls;
> Things of this world, to die are doomed
> but beauty is perpetual."

After showering and then sharing lunch with Mom - who had waited for him - he thanked her and went out under a rainbowed sky and walked a couple of blocks over to Morgan's house, where he told her about his discovery. She was very interested, but kept silent and told no one else besides. And although Mom also kept the secret, and even though no one else happened meanwhile to stumble upon the little Faery door in the elm, by the next day hundreds of people had heard about it. It may be that there just aren't really any secrets, especially with all these willows whispering away.

The word spread, and the tale seemed to change and grow with the telling. Some heard that a family of djinn who had fled the war-torn Middle East had moved in. Some heard that a gnome had taken up residence in the elm, and that he was renting it from the elves who asked only that he feed the squirrels each day. Some warned that the faeries would snatch children away to the Faery land of Tir Na Nog, where they would never be heard from again, except on Midsummer eve when they might be seen dancing in a ring with the faery rascals who had taken them.

Most people, whether they believed in it or not, heard the news and even the warnings with delight and curiosity. But one fellow was particularly displeased to hear of the tidings. He stood at his high office window downtown, caressing his curly black beard and staring out at the night. The stars over the Twin Peaks were shining merrily, but all he could see was doom.

VIII. The Light

Hylos the sun drove the flame-maned horses of his fiery chariot, mounting the sky high over Gaea the earth who watched his glorious ride in mellow adoration and hovered 'round him - like luminous faeries spinning in constant song.

Of course she thought that most of what she'd said over the many years was lost in the bright howl of his flames, but his light brushed over every one of her words of ferns and waterfalls and birds and trees and clouds and cliffs as she turned.

While he was yet ascending, down in the grove the regular Tai chi class was in session, its students moving in unison sundances of rhythmic symmetry. Tourists wandered through, looking for the next attraction on their maps, while nannies pushed strollers around as usual. But they all were also noticing an unusual stir around the grove which was spreading out beyond it in waves of wonder.

A small band of children ran among the trees, looking for one not far from the fountain, with the little door at its base. They found it without much difficulty, as someone else had already tied a green ribbon 'round the trunk of the elm to mark it. They knelt down, gently knocked, and shyly opened the door. Although the light and music were quiet now, the magic was present, and the children gazing inside were roused with waking memories, and they lead some more children as well as a few adults back over to the little door. A mockingbird perched nearby was weaving their laughing chatter into his song.

By the next day, people were coming from all around the city to witness the magic, standing in line to take turns peering inside and wondering and discussing whence this little miracle had come. Some wrote messages of welcome and of wishes, asking for answers and advice on various things, and they left the notes inside the door along with little gifts of seashells, eucalyptus buttons, small woodcarvings, feathers, bouquets of tiny wildflowers, dream catchers, coins, and other such items. Some adorned the tree with braided twine, hanging pine cones and crystals and daisy chains.

And listening from the cozy moss carpeted attic of the elm, or peeking from overhead like green leaves dangling in the breeze, faeries were laughing with delight at how their plan was working out. For with just an extra touch of magic they had awakened some people to the magic that had always been present here, and all while remaining invisible themselves.

After the Faery Ring on the night of the moon, some of the fae had worked on the door for the elm, fashioning it out of fallen pine and lost treasures, while some of them gathered and wakened the sleepy dandelions to catch the starlight, and others arranged a chorus of butterflies whose rare song was taught to them as they all lay in wait within the hollow bole of the tree.

They released all this sorcery when that boy had opened the door, and their laughter was then and even now as the bright bell notes and clear water voices of the robins when at Winter's end, the buds are shooting from the waking boughs and the hills are softly burned green.

And just as Spring always brings new adventures, on they came.

One of the Many Sprites of Spring

IX. Tuesday Afternoon

The following Tuesday after school, the playground was full of great drama. Alien pirates had kidnapped Joan of Arc, but their ship was now being attacked by the ghost of Julius Caesar. A magnificent band of adventurous heroes were crossing a great fiery river of hot lava by means of the hot lava boots they wore, and a Highlander marched by playing the bagpipes, accompanied by Pan the forest god playing on mellower pipes of his own, while a stampede screamed past them, being chased by the Barf Monster.

Rio and his friend Morgan sat under the maples near the long slide. He was reading aloud a scene from Shakespeare's Midsomer Nights Dreame - the one in which Oberon and Puck are discussing their plan to lead two human duelists astray in the fog and away from their foolish battle:

"*Puck:*
'My fairy lord, this must be done with haste,
For night's swift dragons cut the clouds full fast,
And yonder shines Aurora's harbinger;
At whose approach, ghosts, wandering here and there,
Troop home to churchyards: damned spirits all,
That in crossways and floods have burial,
Already to their wormy beds are gone;
For fear lest day should look their shames upon,
They willfully themselves exile from light
And must for aye consort with black-brow'd night.'

Oberon:
'But we are spirits of another sort:
I with the morning's love have oft made sport,
And, like a forester, the groves may tread,
Even till the eastern gate, all fiery-red,
Opening on Neptune with fair blessed beams,
Turns into gold his salt green streams.
But, notwithstanding, haste; make no delay:
We may effect this business yet ere day."

Morgan listened, watching the leaves dancing in the light, and preferring not to play any of the parts herself. So often had her teachers, parents, and even some psychologist demanded that she stop dreaming and speaking of Faery tales, that now she preferred not to talk much at all. Rio was one of her few friends in their second grade class. Her hair was sun gold, her eyes sky blue, and her spirit was like a mountain lake in the morning - quiet, reflective, and deep.

She and Rio looked out toward the North as a procession of white whales soared high above, migrating out toward the ocean sky.

One of the hot lava daredevils, who had then become one of the Barf Monster's quarry running by, stopped as he saw Rio and Morgan gazing skyward, and he watched the whales for a moment with them. His name was Omar and he was friends with pretty much everyone in their class. His hair was dark and curly as a lamb's wool, his skin deep earth brown, and his eyes were like a clear Summer night. These three children all lived over in the Mission District and had walked down to Golden Gate Park from their school so they could all ride home with Omar's moms who would be picking them up there.

"Come and get chased by the Barf Monster!" Omar said, trying as usual to spur these other two into some action he found more interesting.
Rio shook his head. "I'm reading right now," he said.
"But I think he actually did barf!" said Omar.
Morgan gazed back and forth at the two, like someone watching a tennis match with mild interest.
"I want to read up on the faeries," Rio told him. Then Omar remembered the news of the mysterious little door that Rio had found a few days earlier. His tone softened.
"Will you show me the Faery Door?" he asked. He looked over at the old iron sundial. "We have time before my moms get here," he said.

So Rio and Morgan got up and the three kids walked back through the trees and along the trail Rio knew, past lawns, through thickets, and into the elm grove. Along the way, Omar realized it was farther than he had thought, but he was too eager to see the Faery Door by now to suggest turning back.

They neared the elm but had to wait in line to look into the door. Two other kids in line were arguing about the difference between an elf and a faery. Rio told them that back when the fabric of the English language was being woven out of Norman French and Anglo-Saxon, the terms were used quite synonymously, but "Faery" was also a more general term, referring to the whole realm of natural magic. He directed them to Chaucer's Canterbury Tales for an example of usage, and in particular to the prologue of the Tale of the Wyfe of Bath. The other kids looked at him warily, as if he had come up suddenly and begun speaking in tongues. Seeing he had lost them somewhere, he said more simply, "So 'Faery' means 'magical beings' which includes elves." This they seemed to understand, but after he had turned away he heard them quietly resume their same argument.

This was Morgan's third visit to the elm, and she stood looking at it in quiet reverence. Omar gazed around in wonder at the radiant peace of the grove.

When their turn came they saw the gifts and the pile of notes which people had left there for the Faery folk. Rio, who loved reading everything from cereal boxes to encyclopedias, took out and read a few of them. The first was neatly written in pink pencil:

"Dear Faery,
Why did you put this door here?
Love,
Sofia"

The next one was printed in green crayon:

"Dear Faery,
Please enjoy the candy I am leaving for you.
Take small bites because you are very small.
From Nikko"

Omar looked in again and found a half eaten piece of hard candy and a snail who was almost too chubby for her shell.

And there was this one in blue pen:

"Dear Faeries,
I have come here three times but you are never home or maybe you're hiding. Why can't I see you? I am very nice.
Love, Ashlee"

"Hey, I know her!" Omar said.

The next note said:

"Dear Faery,
Do you have any pixie dust? If you do, would you sprinkle me with some?
Love, Quinn"

And there was this one:

"Hi Faeries,
Please let me know how to tell someone that I like him without having my heart crushed into little tiny pieces of sadness. Thanks and have a fabulous day.
Love, Andrea"

For Morgan, who had always been fascinated by Faery magic, but too often ridiculed by those who pretended it didn't exist, the marvel of the Faery Door was a good hint that she had always been quite right.

She found a bit of purple crayon and silently wrote on a piece of paper she took from her small notebook, a message of her own:

"I believe in you.
Love, Morgan"

Rio felt the gratitude in her words as he read them out loud before placing her note into the tree with the others. As they stood to leave, he heard a sound which was maybe some water coursing up through the tree's roots and trunk and out to the leafy limbs held wide, and which seemed to him to be saying, *"Thanks. We believe in you too."*

No one else seemed to have noticed though. Morgan's gaze was now streaming along the path of the glowing clouds as she trailed behind Omar who had put his hot lava boots back on and was striding through the falling light. Rio looked again at the tree who just continued to stand there contentedly while another group of kids studied her door, and then he turned and walked after his friends.

The sky was ripening to flame. The gliding whales had passed the Farallon Islands and were reaching the edge of the world where the sky and sea blend into one boundless depth. A band of fiery red Ohlone Indians were tracking them westward into fading glory as the Mission bell tolled seven times - it was only six o'clock, but occasionally Saint Francis will wander through the city (which he had long ago seen in a distant vision) and give the bells an extra chime.

One of the Ohlone scouts turned to grace the wind with a song of broken light. Here is a translation of one of its shards:

> "We stood a while longer
>> under the wind and stars
>> watching the walls
>>> and fences spread;
>> the edge of our world
>> rolling back upon us
>> until the tribes were broken
>> and Coyote in exile
>> fled"

A fair haired child named Danny looked inside the Faery Door to see that all the notes had disappeared, just as Venus turned on her light above to herald the night and her purple legions, and the burning sun slid into the deep sea with a last flash of green - which a few people actually noticed.

And out on the darkened horizon, Drake the pirate and his crew steered the ghost ship of the Golden Hinde on up toward the lustrous beach at Point Reyes, never seeming to notice the lights of San Francisco burning into the night.

DJEMBE

X. Rhythm

The friends walked back along the trail to the playground where Omar's moms were looking all over for them, and they heard a circle of drums as they passed through Sharon Field. The drum voices spoke in rhythm of the tides and the rising moon, the flows of the streets and trails and migrations of the birds, the lighting of candles and the evening star, and the rise and fall of civilizations. The drummers wove the rhythms into geometric trails which the children followed and saw a thousand moonlit moths beating their rock dusty wings; they saw landscapes of turquoise rains and stars opening in bloom like the daisies that the faeries sometimes left aglow all night; they saw the seasons run like beautiful verses of an eternal song; and they saw the river of Time flowing out of and ever returning to the Timeless Sea.

In the twilight they heard the drummers chanting of Gaea and the opening sky. And Diana, the old one who played an African djembe, sang of the world beginning not with a big bang, but with a big beat which flung and scattered the first stars into space to bring day to all the new worlds emerging out of Chaos and into the great dance.

And she sang the ancient song of Eurynome the nymph who, dancing naked over the waves, had kicked up the wind which she rolled between her hands to form Ophion the serpent who married her; then Eurynome became a dove and laid the World Egg, around which Ophion coiled until out from it hatched all the moons and stars and planets, including the earth, whose name is Gaea, born of the cosmic wind and waves, and still spinning upon them.

A few of the Lost Children who made their camps among the tangled bushes and fallen trees, and who roamed the ivy knotted trails which only they and the other wild creatures of the park knew, moved among the starlit wood with the patterns of sound. One of them was a fellow named Pan who never speaks a word but often plays among the kids in the playground, pretending to be one of them who is pretending to be Pan the forest god in whose yellow eyes can be seen the soul of the wilderness. He played on his shepherd pipes, calling the West Wind into the dance.

The three friends danced too, chasing one another over the moon-glossed grasses.

At the playground they begged Omar's moms to let them play for five more minutes, but were soundly refused, loaded into the red van, and strapped in perhaps a bit more forcefully than usual, and a little tighter than necessary, Rio thought.

Taken home and each set free to dream, they dreamt of the faeries whose eyes were suns of sentience, fluttering around a ring of drumming California Indians, while the dandelions were sprouting up wherever their own dancing feet touched upon the grass, the seeds with their cargos of hope sailing out on the wayfaring solar winds, scattering life far and away over the Mountains of the Moon and the turquoise sands of Ceres.

And here the dreaming diverged: Omar drifted in the path of the floating seeds, seeing them bloom into stars; and Morgan saw the moon weeping tears of pearl, imploring her mother the earth to awaken and hold her again; while Rio was being chased by the giant galactic barf monster - one of those dreams in which you're trying hard to flee but your sneakers keep slipping on the Milky Way. He had glimpsed a distant vessel under full sail, coursing out on the cosmic winds, but then he lost it in the crowds of stars.

DANDELION

XI. Fame!

Reporters began to show up around the elm grove, pushing through the crowds, interviewing folks and filming the general commotion. Their stories of the mysterious Faery Door of San Francisco spread around their networks, and soon became international news, and in many languages were the various translations for the word "faery" being mentioned on television and printed in newspapers ("hada", "vila", "aljanna", "tunder", "fata", and "twylyth teg", to name a few). But the focus of most of these news stories was not so much about faery lore, or magic, but about how the people of San Francisco had finally gone completely crazy.

Even so, many were inspired to come from their far away shores and see the Faery Door for themselves. While the notes to the faeries continued to stack up in the hollow of the tree, some of them were now in foreign tongues, and coins from other nations began to show up as well. The lower boughs of the elm were draped in silk banner from some distant land, and strange rune carved stones appeared around her base.

The field mouse sprite and his snail had decided to take up residence in her hollow trunk and collect the piles of notes at the end of each day. They and sometimes a friend or two would pull them up into their hidden woody attic and admire them by the soft green light of the vibrant moss. None of the faeries could read the writing, but they liked all the fancy marks people were making just for them.

Nor could they of Faery understand any of the varieties of speech people used when calling to them to come out and get their picture taken, but even had they been able to make sense of those encoded syllables, they still would have held to the vow they had made long ago - to remain unseen. For an age had they dwelt under the veil which Gaea and Hylos had been helping them to spin from their patterns of texture and color. Rarely, during the times when the veil was most thin (Midsummer eve, the Harvest, the Yule, and on the first fires of buds) some human out wandering the seam of shadow has stolen a glimpse of Faery, but usually only those just newly arrived to the world may see the gentle flashing of soft colors as they croon and chatter in their cribs at night.

The elm became as reverently ornate as any of her ancestors of antiquity and legend: Merlin's Oak; the Golden Bough which stood by the ancient, arcadian lake known as Diana's Mirror; and old Yggdrasill the great Ash whose roots were said to be supporting the earth. And for a moment she wondered if her fellows in the grove might become jealous of all the attention and admiration being given her; but they only sighed contentedly in the mild afternoon breeze and reminded her that a tree will always do its very best to take stoically anything that comes her way, be it favorable or unfavorable. They stirred their limbs in the warm sunshine, saying that if anything they were proud of her but that she might want to fortify her bark a bit, to protect it from all the brushing hands.

And the elm looked down upon the familiar trio of children sitting at her base, one of them as usual reading some of the messages from inside the door while his friends listened and laughed, and she blushed a deep, vibrant green out to the tips of her heart shaped limbs.

Rio and Morgan and Omar were laughing with a note which had been written by a kid named Benny who had the audacity to ask the faeries for a lifetime supply of gumballs, a pony who was brown but could become invisible too, and a time machine.

High over the Golden Gate, the half moon lingered like a stepping stone in a blue sea of light.

Aengus, the Wanderer

XII. The Rose

Summer comes leisurely over the golden coast, rinsing the hills to blonde and dazzling the waters with reflections of Summers past. The meadow faeries open the roses to flood the air with a deep tide of desire.

As this morning gently stirred, the ladybugs were swarming over the tall drying grasses like hot embers over amber flame. The trees were in lush full bloom. Robust green and fully armed, the spiky, purple thistles dared anyone's grasp.

The old windmills stood abandoned on the shore, letting the waves of fog glide right through their idle arms.

By the Angler's Lodge, a young father was teaching his younger daughter how to cast a flyrod and she was discovering that he was not an expert either, yet still they both enjoyed rippling the reflections of the pines in the casting pools.

They heard from overhead the vivid chatter of the parrots, all descended from the mythic pair whose green wings had transcended the cage.

Ever hoping to feel the warm rains they knew only from their tropic dreams, a new brood was learning to fly, soaring through the foggy woods and over the sea-weathered blocks of crouched rooftops.

A woman whose long tresses of russet red were hanging low, sat by the Faery Door, weeping for her family and writing a prayer for peace.

It was a morning full of beauty, as have been all mornings since the shy awakening of the first dawn who brought with her the light of a million roses.

Windmill

XIII. Sunshine and Shadow

In front of the Botanical Gardens a beech tree unfurled its sculpted limbs, catching the narrow beams of the sun shining through the misty white veil. A young man was sitting on the grass to read beneath the bronze boughs. The article on the screen of his electronic gadget was concerning the faeries of San Francisco and had been published by the news network known as the Inquisitor. He frowned in worry as he read.

The article said that not only were the faeries in the country illegally, but that being invisible they were likely suspects for many of the unexplained catastrophes of history, and now that they seemed to be getting bolder in making their presence known, they would not likely stop at merely vandalizing one tree. It said that already there had been a rise in reports of things like power outages, missed buses, runaway dogs, runaway cats, runaway wives, illegal campfires, and socks disappearing out of the clothes dryer. This story, along with others published on the same day about wars being fought to maintain the peace, about the sun being fated to someday burn out like a cheap lightbulb, and about the grocery stores selling food made entirely out of plastic and sawdust (granted, some of them actually were), had but one general message: "Be afraid."

And while the voice of fear may often sound wise, if given its way it would sacrifice wisdom and all other virtues upon an imaginary altar of Safety.

So while the friends of the Faery Door yet continued to expand in number, there was also a growing clamour for its destruction. The Police Department and City Hall began to receive calls and letters about the Faery Door being a public nuisance. These mainly anonymous complaints stated, among other things: that the poor elm tree would be harmed by all those hippies hanging around it and stuffing it with messages; that having something so inspiring on public property was unfair to those too shallow to believe in anything; that it was influencing people's minds into false happiness; and that the faeries were indeed stealing socks out of people's dryers.

The fear spread like fungus creeping through a dark wood. Quite a few of those who initially were delighted upon hearing of the Faery Door now began to doubt whether it was a good thing. Fortunately, just as fungus will not take over a thriving tree, those who had actually gazed into the door were not much swayed by the ripples of doubt, for nothing can drive away the dark shadows like laughter. Most of these were children, whose dreams are still green limbed.

But watching these things transpire, the blue faery was worried - for she had seen other times when such shadows had grown over the land, instigated by a form of magic the faeries did not possess: Words - the words of the human folk.

And she remembered well the tragic results.

XIV. All Good

Evening loves to lean down like a mother with a softly sung lullaby. She smoothed the sea and pulled the sky over the beds of forest and field and town.

In a clearing amongst the towers of dark leaves, a small choir of pale hawk-feathered faeries with tresses fair as moon, howled their wordless greetings in voices of singing wind to each waking star.

The shaggy shadows of the buffalo hunkered in their dusky pasture, softly grunting to one another through the twilight, while dragonflies crouched quietly beneath lacy ferns among the braided boughs of the slumbering tea trees.

The cypress trees stood against the edge of the world, listening contentedly to the hushing surf rolling into the dark shore.

People gathered together under their roofs and tents, sharing fire and dreams.

It was all good.

Even in times of gathering trouble and trash, beneath it all, the world is actually still clean.

Cypress

Tea Tree

XV. Birth

The moon was a bright beacon amongst schooner clouds sailing over the deep indigo night, and she doused them in white fire, sending their shadows gliding across the grass down near the Pioneer Cabin, where all the faeries of the area were gathered in the field of shifting light and darkness.

Some stood holding hands and some hovered, all in a ring of glowing bloom over a patch of clover, and sang in the soft somber tones of the Mourning Doves, and the sun-faded hues of Summer's end, each taking a verse in turn.

Hovering near the shadow of the hickory tree, her deep sea eyes containing both wild storm and calm, the blue faery with wings of clear water sang of ancient days:

"It was a dark web of words, which ages ago had led to our exile.
I remember the mad crowds who drove us from our lairs with their axes and fires of judgment.
And even some of the people, the wiser ones whom they named the Witches and the Saints, they locked up or murdered just for being our friends."

And the hawk feathered fae then chorused the vow they had all made in those days:
"To dwell in the wilds between light and shadow, invisible as the winds, never to show ourselves again to those foolish mortals - until the day when: the silent heart should speak;

the sun stands still over the horizon; and the deepest shadow glows like a swarm of stars."

A doe was foraging among the tender leaves of the Poison Oak at the foot of the lush hill, and listening to the Faery song. And in the circle, the deer faery took up the next verse, of the current age, her antlers flashing white in the moonglow:

"But we have challenged the darkness again; and we drove back the shadows for a time, by flinging open the little door to our realm - into which the people may see but not tread. And now the darkness challenges us back."

"I knew it would not be easy," said the green faery with wings like willow leaves, *"for when the moon gave us this task, she wept."*

"I thought she wept for the earth as she often does," said the one who resembled a Painted Lady butterfly, with a crown of orbiting embers.

"She weeps for us too," said the blue faery, floating there like an indigo tear of the feathered sky, *"for she knows that the only way to conquer a tide of words is with more words, but while the words of Faery are of wind and earth, and of sky and fire, the words of humanity are so hollow and strange that we of the fae have never been able to grasp them well enough to use."*

A dark eyed faery with wings like starry midnight said he thought that even most people didn't understand their own words very well, which was why they could be so entranced by them.

"With words," he said, *"the people may sculpt their histories into strange shapes, whereas the history of the faeries is written in the patterns on the barks of trees, the ripples of the windswept dunes, the contours of the hills, the tapestries of clouds and the orchestrations of the stars. So of course, our trying to engage them in speech would be futile."* This faery, long ago in a faraway land of frost, had been known as "Loki".

"Let's just close the door," he said. *"They will soon forget all about it, or turn it into another bedtime story. They'll forget about us again, and about the magic of which we and they too are made. And we will go away, back out to the great forests where many of our other kin still dwell - they who have never even seen a human, although they've heard the trees whispering of the ones who make the great smokes. Far away from them, we won't be tempted again to rouse these lost souls who seem determined to stay lost."*

"It would be nice, far away from the crowded streets, not having to stay under veil," said the Painted Lady, *"but if we left now, the shadows would only continue to grow over the earth, and eventually find us again."*

"We have to continue the plan given us by the moon - somehow," sang the sunset faery. *"The thrush returns not to the egg; nor the oak to the broken acorn. There is no going back. Once the seed sprouts it is bound to bloom."*

"Yes... but how?" sang the green faery with wings like leaves of willow. *"The oak reaches high, but only in the*

light. We need to see the way."

"I have been thinking," said the little sprite with the black eyes and soft fur of a field mouse, *"that if we could only understand and then answer those notes we've been getting at the Faery Door, then the people could hear what we have to say, and know the cargo of our hearts. And realizing who we really are, they would no longer have to fear us for what we are not."* He was a logical one.

"But who's going to read the notes," laughed the faery of the purple thistle, *"you or the snail?"*

"We need an interpreter of some kind," answered the sprite.

"We need a poet," sang the blue faery. *"Among those who use the speech of men, we do understand but those who speak from the heart, for the heart always speaks in rhythm."*

"Who actually does that anymore?" said the dark one with wings of the starry night. *"And even if they did, who among them would also understand our speech?"*

"It's true," she acknowledged, *"there are very few true poets left in the world, and I know of none since the one called Yeats who could also understand the Faery tongue. And that one has long ago crossed over into the wordless realm, to rest in the twilit evergreen hills of his homeland. Nevermore since have we heard from the poet of the Seven Woods."* She pronounced the name of *"Yeats"* with a little eurhythmic dance to a verse of one of his songs:

"O chestnut tree, great rooted blossomer,
Are you the leaf, the blossom, or the bole?
O body swayed to music, O brightening glance,
How shall we know the dancer from the dance?"

"We should have tried this when that poet was still around," she sang. And her blue eyes were vast seas as she stated that they had no one to speak for them.

The little sprite tried to cheer her, reminding them that there was a word they had learned from that poet - one of the most beautiful words of all. The blue faery smiled sadly, saying that although it was lovely, it was just one word, and the human heart rarely used it anyway.

"What about Pan of the Wood?" asked the sunset faery. *"I know he hears us, and sometimes I think he sees us despite our veil."*

"Yes," said the blue faery, *"sometimes he can. But he is as much skilled in human speech as are the new babes who also sometimes glimpse us, but could not tell anyone of it either - until they have become too old to remember."*

"I like the drums in the field, and the grey one who chants with them," sang the fiddler faery, her eyes glittering like galaxies. *"What about her?"*

"I like her too," sang the blue faery. *"But while she sings our lore of trees and skies and winds, she knows not our tongue - her songs have come down through the ages from before the fall."*

"Let us not lose hope," urged the antlered faery - long ago known to the Ohlone tribes as Chamas of the Deer. *"Listen to the prophecy in our vow - we will again have our day in the light, once its three points come true."*

"Then we must needs be patient forever!" snarled the purple thistle. *"Why would the sun ever stand still?"*

"Or the deepest shadow shine like the stars?" agreed the dark one, named Loki in the old tales of fire and serpent and mistletoe. *"Why did I ever make that vow?"* he spat. *"I would have been better off to battle those hordes of lost souls with their fire and axes! I could have completely vanquished them!"* He roared into the flashing moon. A pale spider hung from the hawthorn, and a rat nosed out of its hole near the cabin, sensing death drawing near, and thus a chance to feast soon.

"Loki..." spoke the blue faery - whom he had known ages earlier when she had been one of the Valkyrien, *"the reason why you and we all chose exile instead of war, is that despite everything else, we are still kin with those fools, and love them even now."*

Loki gnashed his glittering teeth.

The moonlight and shadows washed over the faeries now chorused in lively woe. As they sang and wailed like dark owls, a star broke loose and fell through the crowds of constellations from where she had been watching and listening, down through the moon glow and fleet clouds to the meadow floor, landing in a small flowery blaze near the gathered faeries who watched bright eyed as the new faery took form, stood and opened her eyes of starry sentience.

And in a voice like the night wind, she sang of the little boy who had first discovered their door and who sometimes came with his friends to read the notes left there by other people, and whose speech she could hear because he spoke from the heart.

"I know of whom she speaks," said the field mouse sprite. *"The boy with the eyes of unfathomable depths who comes to the tree. A poet he may be, for occasionally I've heard his talk, and have known its meaning. And one day I answered in jest, with the water coursing through the tree, and for a moment I thought he might have heard it."*

"We have to find this lad," sang the blue faery. *"We can test him to see if he does hear our words; and if he can, and is indeed a poet as well, he may be able to speak for us."*

"I once heard his song of stars and sea," sang the new one of the night wind. *"He gave it out to the night, and my sisters and I blushed to hear it. Perhaps this is Yeats, the poet of the Wild Swans, returned. But whether it be he or no, this is a true poet; and if he actually does have the speech of the fae as well, then certainly such a one could interpret our message, and burn through the dark web of human words woven 'round Faery since the fierce hours of the witch hunts."*

The other faeries smiled and fluttered 'round her,

singing like nesting doves. They clothed her in clover and a twined crown of hawthorn berries, and gathered her into their family.

Somewhere over in the Richmond District a baby giggled.

Mandwan,
the Moth-Winged
Autumn Leaf
of the Sunset's Hues

XVI. The Calling

Shadows of the trees grew long, stretching their limbs out over the lawns. Drifting from the woody boughs above, falling leaves met their shadows which came gliding across the grass to catch them. The little faery of the sunset's hues was hanging out in the maple tree near the trail which runs between the playground and the elm grove. He was enjoying the leaves and shadows but he had come there to find the little poet who had knocked first upon the Faery Door last Spring. His eyes of deep magenta kept watch.

Children and parents and dogs and dog catchers had been running by all afternoon, but the faery waited until he saw the boy whose eyes were windows of deep soul come running up the trail with his two friends: one whose skin was brown as the heart of the earth, and the other whose hair was as golden as the horses of the sun.

Watching them, the faery admired human friendships and their likeness to Faery friendships. And he thought about some of his most favorite friends: the blue faery with her wings of clear waters - who long ago in a far green country had been known as Aethas of the Birds, just as he in this land had been named as Mandwan the Burning Bush; and the field mouse sprite - who had never by any tribe or nation of people been named; and Gaea and her wild soul of green; the wandering Aengus; the little moths who flickered in the moonlight; the gentle giant oaks; and long, long ago - before the witch hunts had driven them apart - the human child who sang with Faery.

He wondered where the spirit who had been that child was now as he sailed along like a drifting Autumn leaf, keeping in front of the sun so the three children would not notice his stalking them. Being of similar color and material, while skipping along the copper sun rays, he did not cast a shadow. He danced among the other drifting leaves, and he wished that more people could recognize all the real friends they do have - and enemies too.

A breeze arose as the children stepped into the Memorial Grove. They walked through the evergreens and golden halls of oaks which were fountains of falling leaves all glowing like embers of setting sunfire. The faery saw dancing with gentle playfulness around them the young ghosts with solemn eyes and mellow hearts.

They passed a cromlech in the wood, made of stones that had been brought over from the ruins of a 12th century Spanish monastery, crossed the road and strolled past the Academy of Sciences, and then wended their way through the wood to the Faery Door. Not many other people were around.

Omar reached into the doorway and gathered a small stack of notes some people had left for the faeries despite the recent warnings. Morgan examined some of the latest offerings left there for the Faery folk: a Chinese coin which had a square shaped hole in its center; a pine cone; a sand dollar; a plastic seahorse and a tiny toy hammer. Omar handed the stack of notes to Rio and sat down against the tree to hear him read.

The sunset faery met with the blue faery and the field mouse sprite, who had been waiting amongst the elm's turning leaves.

"That's him!" softly sang the sprite upon seeing the boy, and the three faeries were excited to note that they could hear his dreams and desires when he spoke. And now they were about to weave their speech around him, and to watch and see whether he actually could understand them too.

The short note on top of the stack was from a young boy. Rio read:

"Dear Farrys,
I wish that I will not die til age a hundred.
Love, Sunil"

He shuffled to the next note in the stack, but before he could begin to read it, he saw a golden leaf break from the elm and turn red before it wafted out of sight on the somber breeze; and from the tall cypress in the distance, where the peerless Phoenix had built his nest, he heard a song of praise for the setting sun which then engulfed the whole cypress in its glare.

Rio looked at Morgan and Omar to see if they had noticed what the faeries had just said.

"What's up?" Omar asked him. The light from the falling sun blushed his deep brown skin and glimmered among his curly black faux-hawk.

"They answered the note - the one I just read!" said Rio. They can understand me, and I can understand them!" He was fascinated with the discovery of a new language.
Morgan watched him intently, holding aside the sun washed hair from her clear-eyed gaze.
"What did they say?" Omar asked.
Rio thought for a moment, calling up his words into the best interpretation he could, and shared:

"Dear child... We do no counting with your numbers, but this is what we hope for you: that when you are ready to move on to new fields of dreams, you will do so with as much hope and wonder as you had coming in to this one. Love Faery."

Morgan smiled. She liked these faeries.

The three faery friends above chattered like excited sparrows, so much so that a blue feather fell from their conversation.

"They seem pretty cool," said Omar, "but why are they giving us the answer to that message - do they want us to find Sunil and tell him what they said?"

Rio saw the little feather drift down, and then he heard a raven growling from the dark thicket over by the Shakespeare Garden, and a moment later saw

Venus turn on overhead. The stars were still hidden but little glimmers rippled the dusky sky at the points where they would soon be glaring brightly.

"Oh," Rio said with some concern. "I think... yeah - they want me to be the interpreter between the realms of Faery and Humanity so that we can save the world."

"Awesome!" said Omar. He watched Rio who did not appear very enthused. "...isn't it?" he asked him.

"Not sure," said Rio. "I've never tried saving the world before."

He had been worried about his dad, from whom they had not heard a word in many months; and feeling now the whole weight of humanity upon him, and hearing the harsh call of duty, he looked searchingly up among the boughs of the elm, its annually trimmed limbs raised like fists swaddled in deep green and gold, and he asked softly, "Couldn't someone else do it?"

Omar and Morgan watched and waited, listening but hearing nothing unusual. The elm stood unwavering. Looking around the dusky grove, Rio saw the last shadows of the trees entwining over them like a cage. And over at the bus stop by the museum, a few people waited in silence, too full of doubt to be anything more than strangers in the waning light as the clutching shadows covered them too. He sighed. "Alright, I'll speak for you."

From the leaf lush tree top, the three faeries peeked down happily at the boy like waking stars.

Rio looked at Omar and Morgan, and as he saw that both of them were willing to help too, he felt the weight diminish somewhat. He smiled as the shadows flooded them in dusky violets.

As they were walking back to the playground, the South Wind brushed past them and wheeled around the great cypresses on the lake shore. Having crossed deserts of bone and ash, rivers of stones all singing in colors, and a border that was nothing to her but a line in the sand, this clear current carried a scent of dreams to one of the green parrots soaring over the trees, who then turned her gaze and spirit down the far blue coast, and broke away from the flock.

The Cromlech

XVII. Storm

The somber sky was the smoldering ember of a blue flame. Out beyond the Farallon Islands, the swells of the deep sea arose in lucent green, striving to touch the dark Titan, but always breaking. Enraged by the bonds of gravity, they threw themselves belligerently onto the wind, and reared up in monstrous fury.

The snow-breasted gulls felt the angry gusts around their wings and yielded to the looming sky, roughly gliding in towards the steadier shore. Watching them leave the open, the sailors steered their vessels farther out beyond the breaking of the tempest, skipping like thrown stones over the pounding tumult on their white canvas wings.

The selkies, who appeared as seals, but were spirits who had once upon a time been human (just as some of the white gulls were actually the spirits of sailors who had drowned at sea, the selkies were the souls of those who had long strode the shores awaiting their return), now huddled with their seal clans upon the black rocks mattressed with green and purple seaweed, and watched the wrathful swells with their unfathomably deep, dark eyes focused not only on the storm but on eternity as well.

The wind wailed over the desolate isles, resounding like the empty heart of a banshee, but the selkies feared not the Sea Witch nor the storms she now and then hurled upon the coast. They knew she was not evil - it was just that her heart moved through cycles of storm and calm that not even she herself could predict.

The waves rushed and thundered upon the beach in herds of wild white horses. The savage wind lashed through the tall trees, shaking them to their roots, and howled by doors and down chimneys like a pack of ghost wolves. The high brow of the Sea Witch smoldered and flashed, and ripping apart her robes of purple conjured clouds, she released a beating torrent upon the green feathered drum of land.

Although it was just water, most people - including Rio's mom, who wouldn't let him go out either - hid from the great storm under their hammered roofs which were, along with the streets, washed clean.

Rio dreamed of his dad somewhere upon the bucking sea; and the faeries danced with the dark angels of storm, riding the wind and free falling with the wild sprites of rain.

But a few folks out among the swaying trees, turned their faces skyward into the great kiss of Creation. They could not see the faeries but they could feel their anonymous joy.

And afterward, on the night beach lay tons of strewn treasure - shells and sand dollars cast up by the sea. She was not at all sorry or trying to make up for her fury - she just liked to bear gifts for those who still loved her anyway.

XVIII. Stardust

In a shadowy room, high up in the Inquisitor building downtown where the skyscrapers cluster, some people who deal in tangled words were having another table pounding meeting. The black bearded Chief Executive Officer of the Inquisitor News Network and Broadcasting Company was upset over some posters that Rio's mom had printed for the boy and his friends to post in shop windows around the city, announcing the upcoming gathering at the Faery Door. It said that the boy Rio would be serving as interpreter for the faeries who were going to reach out to the people by actually answering the letters they had been receiving.

The Chief Executive Officer - we'll call him "Blackbeard" - was outraged that there would still be this sort of positive interest in the faeries and in the world in general, even after all the extra anxiety they had tried to spread. Their sales had been declining since the Faery Door had been discovered, and Blackbeard was taking it as a personal threat, not merely due to the drop in income, but due to the loss in control over the hearts and minds of people. He and the others sitting there around the large table spoke of getting the city to remove the tree or at least barricade it as a possible danger. They came up with more gossip to publish about the faeries and they argued over whether poisoned honey might be a good way to get rid of them.

As they discussed these things, the air around them

drifted about in clear, fluid currents softly lit by the strands of the setting Autumn sun slipping in past the rain washed western windows and the dusty, dyed curtains. It filled their breasts and nourished their hearts without question - for their hearts were made of the same fire and stardust as anyone else's. And while it may be that some people's basic intentions are simply bad, there is still a boundless beauty in all things - even in the eyes that are blind to beauty.

And ol' Blackbeard was about as blind as they come, for even while his eyes seemed to gaze around the room at the group of corrupt executives, what he actually saw were the shadowy faces of those who had been his henchmen back during that lifetime when he had served as the Grand Inquisitor, trying anyone said to be a witch, and punishing with baptisms of fire those he deemed to be friends of Faery. Covering himself with such dark deeds, his mind was never able to find its way out of and beyond that era. And while recalling a lifetime hundreds of years past would be for most people a sign of waking, in Blackbeard's case it was simply a nightmare from which he had never emerged.

Blackbeard introduced to the others the team of security guards he had just hired to thwart the gathering in the park by preventing Rio from even arriving. The commander of the security force was a large man named D. Goliath whose eyes were hidden by the sunglasses he always wore, even in this dark room. He swore that he and his team would find the boy. "And when we do," he said, "he will know that there's no such thing as magic." Blackbeard almost smiled.

About two thousand miles to the southeast, a lone green parrot was beating her soft wings over the night-raptured desert whose layered sands glittered as a mirror for the constellations grandly sailing over - monuments of the dead, with stars at crest and wingtip. The falling night was full of dreams and remembrance, and her beating heart was full of fire and stardust as she flew.

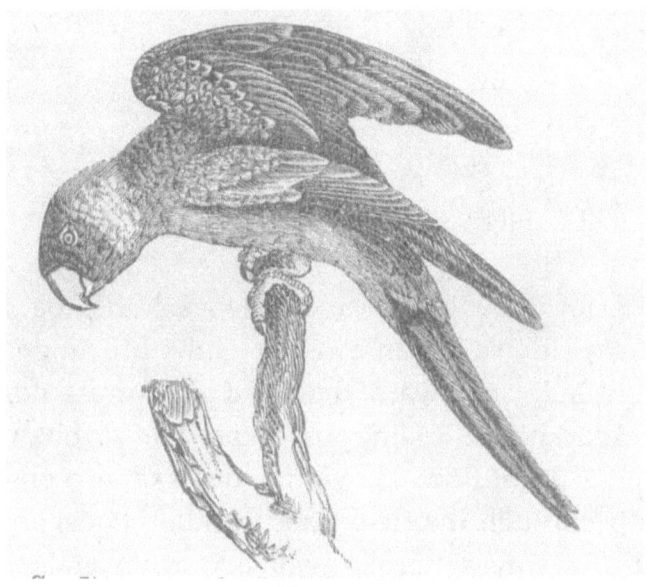

Parrot
From an 1875 Book on Zoology
- Artist Unknown

Above the Fog

XIX. Flight

Called forth by cloudscaped Heaven, the fog rose
over Poseidon's oceanic realm and rode upon the
West Wind, on toward the coast as a great tide of
white darkness. Rolling into shore and through the
Golden Gate, it flooded over the bay and also pushed
silently through the trees and neighborhoods, and in
great slow waves it broke again and again against the
Twin Peaks, finally stacking up enough to spill over
the other side, and in ethereal rivers it ran down over
the slopes of the green grass which the recent rains
had roused.

The trees in the park were dripping with tears, and the leaves of grass hung over with the gathering silver dew. Blackbirds and jays splattered the water drops from the pine and cypress limbs as they fluttered around the area of the grove, alighting and singing happily to one another - excited that the faeries and the people would be coming together this day.

Rio walked with his mom through the mist by the Conservatory of Flowers and crossed the road to take the path through the giant fern forest. Beyond, they started up the knoll of tangled pines and oaks on their way to the elm grove. Each step taking him further into a future he couldn't clearly see, he slowed his pace.

Mom was also looking around for any unusual rock samples but seeing Rio begin to falter and linger, she asked him how he was doing even though she already knew.

Some folks say love is blind but it actually illuminates our senses.

Rio told her that he was feeling a little wary about talking in front of a big crowd. "I want to help the faeries and hear what they have to say, but what if everyone just thinks I'm weird or they get scared and start throwing rotten tomatoes or something?"

Mom listened and then told the boy, "If you keep tomorrow bright in your heart, it will light the path you have to walk today."

Rio listened to the words, and heard along with them - in the calm tone of her voice, the green glow of the grass, and in the quiet roar of the pale fog - this notion also: *"Whatever you may be faced with, you will always have the power to remain yourself. Nothing can ever really hurt you unless you allow it to change who you are."*

He heard the rose horns of the geese, wailing above the white veil. Mom listened too, and pondered also the words she had spoken, and smiled for the future.

His fate decided upon and illuminated, they walked on up the hillside.

Pushing between the low branches of two pines atop the knoll, they were confronted by a large man who stood in the little clearing wearing a black leather jacket and dark sunglasses.

"Hello there," he said smiling, but in a tone that made Rio's mom frown. "You two wouldn't be going down to the Faery Door would you?"

Rio and Mom turned around at the sound of some footsteps behind them to see two more men, both wearing sunglasses and dark trenchcoats, emerge from the drizzle-laden lavender and sage, one of them having to rip his coattail away from a grasping blackberry vine.

"Well, I have to inform you that the party has been cancelled due to the possibility of a riot," said the first man. He showed them his badge and went on to tell them that they were security guards hired by the Inquisitor to protect their reporting staff during these troubled times. "And for their safety and yours too," he said, "we have to take you two into custody for a while." The other two guards began to move up toward them from behind.

Mom was still holding the two low branches, in the midst of pushing through them. She and Rio looked at each other for a moment. Then Rio quickly dropped to lie low on the ground as she pushed through and let go of the boughs which whipped back and slammed into the two men behind, tumbling them down the thorny hillside.

"Go Rio!" yelled Mom as she charged toward the first guard. She was not a large person, but could use well the weight she had, and right now she just hoped to tackle and hold down the big security guard long enough for Rio to escape and reach the Faery Door - at least, it looked to be her intent, although it could well have been pure, primal rage at seeing someone threatening Rio.

She leapt into the big guard, pushing him aside as Rio ran by, but Goliath ducked, turned and flipped her over his arm, sending her crashing into the tangled, snapping twigs of a fallen pine. Rolling over to get up, she noticed an interesting fist-sized stone and her hand automatically snatched it up.

Thinking to lure the big man away from his mom, Rio

shouted as he ran along the trail, "Well, I'm off to the Faery Door!"

Goliath then turned to run after the boy, but at that moment a flock of Canada Geese swooped down, two of them ducking their necks under the running boy's arms, two more falling in to support those, and many more pair taking their places in turn, while a short column of wings stacked beneath his knees as well, all lifting him into their arrow of flight as he held on.

As Rio's mom stood back up, she saw the guard pull a stun gun out of his jacket, kneel and aim it at the flock rising up and away. She was too far off to grab the gun or even to jump in the line of fire, but feeling the solid stone in her hand she swung and hurled it as hard as she could at the guard, just as he pulled the trigger. The electric bolts shot from the gun but instead of forward, they shot to the side to connect with the flying stone, joining it to hit the guard on the head, which knocked him out and layed him down on the wet grass.

Rising wide-eyed toward the West, over the treetops with the honking geese, Rio glanced back at Mom standing near the fallen giant and looking back up at him with wide eyes of her own. One of the geese under his arms pinched his hand in her bill, telling him to relax his grip on her which he did. Mom waved them on, knowing where they were taking him, knowing also that these cowards wouldn't dare to attack him in the grove. And although she thought she ought to feel frantic as her boy was hurling over the trees, her heart was full of exhilaration.

And he enjoyed the beating of wings along their path through the white currents.

Goliath's breathing stirred the mist around the grass. Mom pulled the stun gun from his limp clutch and tossed it into the blackberry bushes. Then she saw and picked up the stone she had thrown. Turning it in her hand, she thought there must be some iron in it for the electric bolts to have been so attracted to it. But looking closer at its shape and grain pattern, knowing that the molecules composing it were little galaxies, each unique and made up almost entirely of free space but all constant in harmonious orbit, she realized that this and all other rocks were the sacred bones of Saint Gaea the Earth.

And she hoped that she and Rio could go rock collecting again soon and that Rio would want to make another labyrinth out of the stones so that this time she could let him, and maybe even join him - maybe even in the rain.

The two other guards stepped through the trees, their wet coats torn and frayed from the blackberry thorns, to see their commander on the ground with a smoking lump on the side of his head, and Rio's mom standing over him with a stone in her hand.

"Magic rock," said Rio's mom, holding it up.
"There's no such thing as magic," said one of the security guards, whose glasses were missing a lens.

They stood looking at the rock though, not wanting to move any closer.

"I'll be going now," she said, turning toward the trail. The two security guards looked at each other frantically.

"Wait! You have Oppositional Defiance Disorder!" said the other guard who was missing both lenses out of his glasses. "I studied psychiatry, and can tell you this is a dangerously unstable and contagious condition, but if you come with us now, we can make sure you get proper care."

Mom started to turn back and say something extremely rude to the guard, but realizing that children may one day be reading this book, she just walked on without another word, following the honking of the geese on toward the grove.

Goliath awoke with a sore head, and as he dizzily sat up on the grass, his assistants told him he had been beaten up by a girl. They had to help him down the hill and to the doctor's office to get his head checked out, and he had to call Blackbeard at the Inquisitor office and tell him that Rio had escaped arrest.

Geese

XX. The Flock

The geese let Rio down unseen on a grassy knoll near the grove, and then they went about their pecking and grazing as if nothing out of the ordinary had just happened. Geese are like that - they may appear frantic or supremely calm, but it is almost always just for effect. And dreaming of new fields in a far green country, the grass and clover without protest let their seeds be plucked and taken.

Rio saw the mass of people among the trees. They were gathered thickest around the barricaded elm, waiting for the event to begin.

Some folks were holding up signs that said various

things - from "FAERY ROCKS!" and "FAERIES, WE LOVE YOU", to "GO AWAY RASCALS!", "NO SUCH THING", and "FAERY IS SCARY". Some reporters were there too, asking people silly questions and taking notes.

Rio walked down into the crowd, weaving around people's legs until he reached the barricade. There were six police officers inside the roped off area, all standing guard around the tree which was garlanded in yellow tape with the words, "CAUTION! POLICE LINE - DO NOT CROSS!" repeatedly printed on it.

Rio looked up into the nearest guard's hard face and asked if he might be allowed to get the notes from behind the little door in the tree. The guard glanced down and said without interest, "There aren't any notes in there."
"Where are they?" asked Rio.
The guard was about to tell the boy to go away, but when he looked down again his stern blue eyes saw that Rio was sincerely interested. And without completely knowing why, he told him, "One of my guys looked in there yesterday and didn't see nothing. And then when he reached his hand in to feel around, something stung him - at least that's what he says. He couldn't see what it was, but his hand swolled up all itchy and red."

Rio said, "Well, that's because he was trying to steal them. I just want to read them like I usually do, so everyone can hear them answered."
The guard shook his head. "No one is going near that

tree until the bulldozer gets here. "The City's already approved its removal. After what happened yesterday, they didn't want any of us trying to take an axe or saw to it, so..." He saw the look of shock on Rio's face. "Sorry, young man," he said, and then turned again to his duty.

While the news of the tree being scheduled for removal was disturbing, Rio kept the future bright in his heart, as his mom had suggested.

Omar and Morgan saw him and came over through the crowd, along with their third grade classmate Claire whose softly brilliant smile was like sun through a silk tree's lacy boughs. She was going to translate Rio's speech into Mandarin Chinese for those who might best understand it that way. Omar would translate into Spanglish. Morgan planned on helping out with whatever else might be needed, as long as it didn't involve speaking to the crowd. She stood by, holding her Tinker Bell thermos which she had bought recently with her own money.

The bell down at Mission Dolores rang three times which meant the Faery conference should be starting around now, but where were the faeries or the notes? The friends stood looking at one another, hoping that one of them would know what they should do.

Then the East Wind began to rise, shaking and loosing the reddening leaves which drifted over the crowd. As the guards gazed upward, the Faery Door opened and Rio saw the notes there which were also snatched up by the wind to mingle with the red leaves and cascade down into the gathering. The children scurried around, gathering the scattered letters, giving their thanks to the people who had caught some of them. The faeries actually could have made all the pages soar directly over to Rio in a neat little pile, but they didn't want to get too fancy yet.

The guards realized what had just happened, but decided to stay inside the barricade and guard the door as their orders had stated.

The crowd made a space around Rio and Morgan who were sorting through the notes, and waited for them to start. One of the park workers came in with a wooden crate and gave it to Rio to stand on. Omar stood a few yards away in the midst of a few Spanish speaking folks, and Claire stood with some Chinese speaking people on the other side of the elm. Rio's mom stood way back in the crowd, up on her toes so she could see.

Rio looked out among the great multitude who seemed so massive and immovable, that his voice seemed to be hiding in some soft chamber of his heart. But a deep breath called it forth, and as he cast it out over the crowd, the daylight purged the shadows from it, and he addressed the people, who quieted to hear him, without faltering at all.

"Alright everyone, we're about to get started. The faeries have some things they want to tell us in answer to the notes they have been receiving from us." Omar and Claire translated Rio's words as he continued. "I can understand the Faery speech, so they've asked me to interpret."

He gazed around at the folks, some of whom he knew he'd never seen before in his life, some regarding him with enthusiasm and expectation, and some with fear and hostility.

Most of them were really just hoping to see a faery with their own eyes, that their eyes might share in what their hearts had always known deep down.

"If you just happened by, you're welcome to hang out with us and hear what they have to say too," he said. And a girl named Harper, who had just happened by and noticed the crowd, decided to hang out with them too.

"I'm actually not sure what's going to happen here today," Rio said to the gathered people, "but we're about to find out." Morgan handed him the stack of wishes, prayers, and greetings written by some of these human people to those others whom they hardly knew as of yet - except from some dreams they had never quite forgotten completely.

XXI. Faery Speech

Everyone was watching and listening to Rio as he read the first note:

"Dear Faeries,
I am Kyle. How are you?
Sincerely, Kyle"

A little boy in the crowd held up both hands in quiet triumph. His name was Kyle, and his mom was a kindergarten teacher. A nearby reporter who was wearing (in my opinion) way too much make up, turned to ask Kyle what he was feeling at that moment, but people around them shushed her. She was actually a very nice person, and I had once thought of asking her out on a date myself, but I just don't think I could ever be more than just friends with someone who wears false eyelashes.

While Claire and Omar were translating for their groups, Rio gazed around the treetops, listening for the faeries. The police guards were glancing around nervously, wishing that dealing with Faery beings had been part of their training. Moments passed. Some of the people began to think that the faeries weren't coming, or wondering whether they had ever really been there at all.

Suddenly the elm tree, seeming to glow with its own deep colors, bowed slightly toward the West, and folded a slender but knarled limb across its middle, sending some more red leaves adrift. Straightening back up, she seemed to stand more stately and ruddier than before.

There were gasps in the crowd, and although Rio had just ridden some geese over the woods, seeing the tree move that way left him speechless for a moment. A soft chorus of voices like a wind in the reeds he could hear, but he just stood watching the elm, his mouth hanging slightly open. The guards had stayed inside the barricade, standing along the inside of the rope, but now instead of watching the crowd, they were all facing the tree, their eyes wide.

Rio felt Morgan nudge his arm.

He shook off his amazement, and interpreted the Faery greeting to the people: *"Hello from Faery! We are artists of the earth and sun, minions of the moon, and we are honored now to make your re-acquaintance!"* The faeries were gathered in the trunk of the elm to sing their verses in turn, with voices of the dew-softened wood and of the feathered wind.

Kyle grinned as his note was answered, and golden light began to reach in through the white fog. Rio took up the next note and read:

"Dear Faery,
Why did you put this door here?
Love, Sofia"

As soon as he finished, he saw a finch's red shoulder feather drifting along on the breeze. It turned and dove and hovered and danced. The bird flew over it and away, singing a melody which sounded something like a tune from Mozart's Magic Flute, but in a different rhythm and scale that had been fashioned through many generations of wings and winds.

Rio interpreted the answer: *"For the same reason you have come to see it, and the same reason the world was made - for fun."*

Some of the crowd smiled at this answer, and wondered if it could actually be true. Sofia, a little girl with crutches and a cast on her leg, laughed loudly - she reckoned that basically it was.

Rio felt every word he spoke, but had to save some of these things the fae were saying to ponder later - for their full meanings were rooted way back in the dim dawnings of time.

He read the next note:

"Dear Faery,
I like your new home. Do you like it too?
Love, Danny"

In answer, the light broke through the fog in many places, shimmering the grove in white and gold. Rio said, *"Actually, our home cannot be shut in by any door nor confined by walls or roofs. Home is the heart, and for that we have not found any borders, however far into the spaces of this world we may look. But yes, we are very* proud of our little door and all the goodness and mischief it has inspired."

The next note said:

"Dear Faery,
I want to know - are you really alive?
From Taylor"

Taylor was a girl whom Omar had met in the park a couple of years earlier. Her parents had come from Brazil, and when she told Omar that she was "Brazilian", he thought she was bragging about her age, and he told her that he was "brazillion and one".

Now Rio heard the chorus of breezes and saw the earth seem to swell as if breathing. He interpreted: *"Yes. We are alive, as is the whole world and everything in it. Even the stones, whose tides of breathing are much slower than yours, are part of the living dream of the world - and some of the dreaming is theirs."*

The misty, golden air was warming as Rio read the next note:

"Hi Faeries,
Where did you come from?
Please answer.
Sincerely, Gavin
PS - I love dogs."

There began a great murmuring of grass and leaves and twigs. The very air around the grove was dancing in small fragrant currents and began to fill with wings.

Starlings and Purple Finches were at play, riding upon the turning air and chasing one another happily.

When this had gone on for some time and did not appear to be ending soon, Rio began interpreting as he continued to watch: *"We awoke with the birth of the stars, amidst their singing and a great chorus of voices laughing and saying, 'Let there be light!' For an age we played amongst the dancing fire. It was tremendous and wonderful - as it still is now, only it was a completely new idea. And some of the ash began to form into wandering orbs of cloud and stone. We found them and woke their spirits of green and they welcomed us in. We have graced Gaea here, and she has inspired us back with life that reaches and falls in grand and simple rhyme. We love her and all that she holds in her blue arms of sea and sky. And like you, our wanderings over her horizons have many times parted and reunited us."*

It was the moth-like faery of the sunset now crying the feathered wind of the next verse. And nodding to Chamas of the Deer, he went on to tell of some of them who had been right here since not long after the ice began to melt from the blue glaciers which had smoothed the flaming mountains of the East after the great feathered dragons had transformed into the birds; when the bay was a rich pasture of bunched grasses through which the shaggy mammoths roamed and the tremendous grey wolves followed in pairs, and through which the rivers of melting ice flowed to tumble over the cliff into the black sea; when strange flowers reached for the white sun and were ravaged by the flame-red bees; when the earth held two moons until one of them broke up in the tides and has since been raining down upon the planet surface each Summer in countless meteors.

As Rio finished interpreting this, from over by the ivy-wound oak wood a coyote pup who was snuggled in his lair and dreaming of trails leading far over the sea after the white sun, yipped in his sleep; and Rio said, *"PS - We love dogs too."*

Rio looked around. The birds had roosted in the trees, and were listening to the long chant and watching with their bright black eyes these human folks who seemed to be growing in wisdom. Most of those who had brought signs were no longer bothering to hold them up. Many people were recording the Faery conversation on their phone cameras, and all were listening intently. It looked to Rio as if the Faeries were reaching folks as they had hoped. He read the next note in his stack:

"I am very sad. Despair has enfolded me and I do not know what to do except to pray that we may stay a family; that the fighting stops and we may live in peace together."

One woman stood listening in stoic silence. her long red hair stirred by the breeze which also swayed the outer limbs of the elms and cast adrift a small fleet of russet-ruby and gold.

Rio watched and interpreted: *"Yes, may it be, for love never dies. It does get cluttered up sometimes like a tree that needs to shake off her dead leaves. But then in the cascade of colors, peace is dazzling and jubilant, rather than as merely the silent sleep of swords."*

The woman breathed deeply, her green eyes clear and serene. The next note was one Rio remembered having read before, from a girl named Quinn whom he had seen in the park and thought she did the best cartwheels in the whole world:

"Dear Faery,
Do you have any pixie dust? If you do, would you sprinkle me with some?
Love, Quinn"

Rio heard little wooden bells of laughter in the chorus, and the trees were burnished in the sunlight. He interpreted: *"Seeing you bake your bread from the grains of grass, we began using pixie dust to make our loaves of light for our Faery feasts. To sprinkle you with it would be the poorest of table manners. But you may feel free to taste it for yourself, for it is abundant. We find it in the first light of daybreak, the last flash of sundown, and all over the leaves on golden afternoons. Flowers catch it in their cups and bees gather it too and there is still much more than any of them could ever need."*

Quinn listened to the answer, amazed, then did a cartwheel on the grass. Rio read the next one:

"Dear Faeries,
I have come here three times but you are never home or maybe you're hiding. Why can't I see you? I am very nice.
Love, Ashlee"

Rio watched a mist glide through the grove and around the elm, thick enough to require looking through its gaps to see the tree. As dead leaves gently rustled over the floor, he focused through the white strands and saw glimpses of the red leafed boughs hanging low over the thick trunk with its weathered bark of knarled patterns. He heard a deep chorus of ancestral voices slowly chanting from the roots of the elms.

And a girl named Ashlee - who really was very kind toward just about everyone - awaited her answer, hoping that it would be simply the faeries revealing themselves; but Rio knew they had something other than their luminous forms that they wanted to reveal. He listened and interpreted:

"Long ago, when we were friends, you watched us turn the seasons, we watched you plant your corn, and our music often mingled in harmony under the bright-souled stars.

Sometimes for fun we pulled the chairs out from your bums, gave your horses the wind as you passed behind, left your goats grazing upon your sod roofs, and hid away one of each pair of your stockings, and such things. But you laughed with us and more loudly, gave us some of your butter and cream, and all was right.

But it came to pass that some of you hearkened the voice of fear who drapes darkness over the night. Through your dark shrouds we were alien, and your fearful words hung dark deeds upon us, including the stealing of your children. But while mischievous rascals we are, never would we have sundered your sacred families.

Indeed, of the spirits among you whose flesh fails their will and too young falls to dust, some then wish to come away with us and are here even now, watching all with Faery eyes. Part of the Faery family are they now, but ever free to part ways or gather among us, as are we all."

The Painted Lady butterfly gazed around at her friends in the elm, watching all with her Faery eyes.

"Even so, you came after us with torches and burned our lairs, and by your axes were our sacred groves felled.

We fled into exile, veiling ourselves from your narrow sight, and left you in your shadows. And like the mole who considers the rose to be but a root, you have ever since been blind to the most splendorous expanses of your world."

Then Rio looked into the tangled boughs of the elm, and asked them, "Why did you have to flee? If you are spirits of light, what harm would you fear from mortal beings?"

The chorus of breezes was very soft. The mist that the elm had caught among her lithe limbs, now fell as lustrous tears which cast the light into shattered rainbows.

Rio took it in and then interpreted for everyone else: *"All that slashing and burning would merely have been annoying to us, for we are unafraid of destruction, and often hold the reins of storm. But having to see - in the eyes that had always looked upon us in kindness and friendship - the cold fires of cruelty... it broke our hearts."*

Rio continued to watch the tree giving its mild rain to the tiny leaves of grass, and also glimpsed faint glows of color around the gathering. Everyone was hushed as he went on:

"In our exile we have continued to regard you and we are amazed by both your grace and folly:

You are as sleeping gods dreaming of a godless world - in which you are but grains of sand upon the shore of an endless sea;
But you are the endless sea, and all worlds are but grains of sand upon your shore;

You are the grace of freedom, whose wild hearts are of fire and stardust;
And yet you weave yourselves cages out of mere shadow and curse your jails;

You think you are hidden under your roofs, from the night which peers down like the dark wolves' eyes;
But aboard this sun showered world sailing through terrible immensity and the unveiled stars, you are on a grand adventure whether your eyes be open to it or not.

We hope you will again awaken - for seeing where you're going, where you've been, and where you are, is much more fun."

Rio then took a moment to breathe and reflect, as did everyone else.

From their veils of wood and light, the faeries gazed on the people, many of whose faces were marked with remorse as they encountered ancient memories they were surprised to have. From behind the lilac hedges, Pan's yellow sunburst eyes saw the ghosts of witch trials and faery hunts falling about the grove to disappear into the light of day.

The faeries serenely forgave the people, the people humbly pardoned the fae, and the water that had fallen, now rose away in white wisps of vanishing steam. Rio watched it flower into clear air as folks quietly gazed upon one another, and then he read the next note:

"Hi Faery,
I wish for a lifetime of happiness for my two girls, Nadia and Ava.
Love, Kara"

Under the soft singing of the Faery choir, the colors of everything gently burned. Rio interpreted:

"We know a parent's love to be the greatest there is. We feel it too - for the grass, trees, birds, air, rain, and earth which we tend and keep. The love astonishes us each hour

of the day and night, because it is much greater than us and yet it is us. And it ties our faery tongues to explain because we create this love and yet it creates us too. We both pity and are glad for you, fellow parent, for we share a joy and sorrow of which there is no greater. And we wish you and your girls much more than happiness."

The next note Rio read was from Omar. The people standing 'round him to hear his translations had to do their best to comprehend what Rio was saying, because Omar was feeling too embarrassed to speak aloud his own message.

"Dear Faery People,
Thank you for bringing all this magic to our world. I see it now.
Love, Omar"

Rio looked around among the trees and birds and people gathered in the grove, but saw no pronounced motion. He listened but heard no voice, but for the tiny cluck of one young finch. All else seemed to be awaiting. Then he understood:

"We appreciate the admiration, but it is also your magic which graces our dreams with beauty, and your ears which grant music to our songs. And even while you folks lie aslumber beneath the burden of darkness, your dreams are commingling with ours to fashion and form the world, but your fears are darkening the dreams of all. We hope you will awaken soon to take rein of your dreams; and that you may again arise to dance over the raging storms of the sun and over the desolation of the night, free of all but the

glorious void of your own freedom."

The afternoon was now sun golden and water blue. Rio was about to read another note when a shadow fell over the elm along with a high pitched whine which scattered the starlings and finches out of the trees and sent them beating their little wings for the edges of the grove. People looked towards the sun and saw what appeared to be a small space ship.

Aethas of the Birds

XXII. Sound and Fury

Blackbeard cursed and threw his phone out of the high window, and then he kicked his rolling chair across the floor and cursed again because he realized he had wanted to make another call. He had just heard about Rio's escape. He grabbed another phone from a lady who wears a dark suit everyday, but then threw that one out the window too, because a better idea came to him. Maybe his hired thugs just weren't very convincing, but he knew of something else that would be. He took the elevator down to the lower garage to get it.

The pale one who stayed down there brought out the van, and then went to get the other thing Blackbeard had asked for - the Inquisitor's secret weapon. Waiting there impatiently, Blackbeard rubbed his black beard and considered his plans. He would use this weapon of spite and thunder upon the gathering in the grove, and he calculated that if it worked well there, he could use it everywhere, and this dark age would never need come to an end.

The van loaded up, Blackbeard drove out through weathered brick-lined streets of smoke and laundry. At a crosswalk, he almost ran over an older lady who shook her bamboo cane at him, yelling curses in Chinese. Sneering at her, he pulled a little notebook from his breast pocket and wrote her name in it. Not knowing her actual name, he merely wrote down, "Mary". She continued cursing him long after he had driven away, and was still at it a couple of hours later while sitting down having dinner with her daughter and grandchildren who got to learn a few new words.

Blackbeard actually got lost in the Haight-Ashbury neighborhood, but eventually recognized the way which led through the dark wood and over to the hedge lined street in front of the Academy of Sciences overlooking the crowded grove. Furtively, he got out and opened the rear doors of the van, then got back inside where he activated the remote controls and sent the large insect-like machine hovering out and over the people and elms. It was a large broadcasting drone with a built in signal jammer, and it overrode all of the phone cameras and other electronic devices being used to record, blacking out their screens and filling the speakers with Blackbeard's monotone growl, while also projecting his amplified words from the steel eyed drone itself:

"Danger! You are all in great danger! Faery is evil! They are taking over the world! They are brainwashing you! Don't listen to them! Run away! Faery is evil! ..."

The great noise was blocking out any possibility of Rio being heard. The friends had no idea who had sent the drone, nor what they might do to get rid of it, so they merely stood by and listened to its rant. The captain of the police guard, with whom Rio had spoken earlier, tried to call City Hall to find out if this was part of some official crowd clearing order, but both his radio and phone would only echo the drone's dire message.

Blackbeard sat in the van nearby, unseen by the mass of people whose attentions were caught up in the snarl of the drone. Seeing a few people abandoning the gathering, he continued to preach his severe warning:

"Danger! Faeries are child stealers! Go home where it's safe and stay there! Take your loved ones and leave before it's too late! Faery is evil!"

The faeries, hearing the persistence of the screeching, decided to call up the wrath of storm. Within the tree, the fae stood in circle, arms reaching toward the center, some with palms turned earthward and some with palms skyward. The blue faery was a raging violet, and the fiddler's eyes were black fire.

The tree began to slowly rock and turn, and a strange music began to be heard, like someone warming up on a tree-sized violin. The mossy hollow within the elm was now aglow with what I call St. Elmo's fire. High above, the winds and clouds began to churn.

There was worry in the air. Folks had a flying machine screaming at them, an unknown number of Faery folk who seemed pretty ticked off, and a strange storm brewing over their heads.

Some of the people were outraged and tried to shout down the noise of the drone, but merely added to it; others were urging calm and patience, and getting into arguments over it. Mom tried to move up to where the kids were, but there was too much noise and confusion in the crowd to get through.

The Faery tune began, seeming to resound in the bones of the earth; and a green flame began to glow around the boughs of the elm, while the music roared like a pride of gryffins defending their cubs, chorused like a thousand avenging angels, and beat like a million wings in battle.

Then from the surrounding oaks and cypress woods came a passionate dancing procession of the Lost Children with Pan and his pipes at the head. They wove through the crowd, motioning folks to dance along with them and the Faery tune, which some did while others began to clap in time.

Seeing the dance, the Faery fiddler gave some bounce to her defiant fugue, turning it into a lively jig, and the people danced along.

Diana, the old one, accented the beat of the Faery tune with her djembe, and infused the air with the fragrance of the Lenke wood from which her drum had been made.

But the rant of the drone overhead persisted, even louder still, and more dire - full of sound and fury.

Morgan watched it hover and shriek, its metallic eye glaring around coldly at those who had the audacity to be alive, and she thought how easy it was for those who have no hearts to torture those who do. But as she took a sip of juice to console herself, the laughter erupted from inside her and came spraying out of her mouth with the juice too. And she laughed in the face of death because behind its mask of grim severity she saw the funny face of life. Those around her were warmed by the mirth, and they began to smile and were soon laughing along with her, and the cheer spread wide as the curtain of fear was torn back.

Even the policemen were chuckling amidst the lifted spirits. The drone was still blasting its litany of terror but no one was any longer under its sway - and the voice was beginning to sound rather frantic.

Then a migration of singing color - the butterflies who had greeted Rio when he had first opened the Faery Door last Spring, and had passed on their song to many others - was now streaming out of the woods and into the open rear doors of the white van, and swarming upon the black-bearded one in the driver's seat who appeared to be horrified by their unearthly song. He scrambled out of the door, swatting at his vibrant, fluttering aura, and Morgan saw that he was holding a microphone. She silently pointed this out to the police captain who then sent two of his guard up to investigate. Seeing them walking toward him, Blackbeard screamed one last volley of fear: "YOU ARE ALL GOING TO DIE!!" but not even the cops were impressed.

The fiddler tied up her tune with a little flourish, and the people ended their dances and bowed to one another, while some watched the scene over by the van. The little butterflies drifted back into the light-dappled woods.

The drone was still running on autopilot, echoing fragments of the phrases it had recorded ("Faery... listen to them... you are all... loved... over the world... you are all... home...") when a lightning bolt struck it from above. It was yanked up and thrown over and beyond the fountain to fall down clanging like an old tea kettle. And the faeries laughed as they had forgotten the storm they had begun to invoke.

Rio noticed the people were turning back toward him again now, and although he thought it quite obvious what the fae had just said, he gave them his interpretation anyway: "Uhh... *'Shut the hell up.*"

The police guards considered taking Blackbeard to jail but they did not wish to leave the grove yet so he merely got a ticket for creating a disturbance. Aroused by the scent of scandal, the several reporters who were there from the Inquisitor besieged the van, pointing their cameras and microphones at Blackbeard, and asking silly questions.

And while all ideas and beliefs are absolutely free, all actions have consequences. Thus, along with the ticket and being hounded by his own press, Blackbeard also noticed when he got home later that evening that all of his socks had been stolen out of the dryer.

Folks quieted down to listen to Rio who was about to

read the next note in the stack, but they were interrupted again, this time by the growl of a tractor which a fellow was driving into the grove. Although earlier they had been dreading this noise, after the battle they had just witnessed, it seemed tame. As the tractor pulled up to the crowd they just stood their ground together. The driver took a look at their unswayable gaze and shut off his engine. The captain of the police guard came over and told him that while he knew there was an order from the city to remove the elm tree, and while an hour before he would have tried to clear the crowd for him, there had been some new developments, and he now considered it his duty to guard the tree from any harm until the city council could meet again and reconsider any actions to be taken concerning it. And he told him to come and join the crowd if he wanted to witness something really cool. And the tractor driver joined the crowd.

Finch

XXIII. Coming Out

The faeries spoke with the people into the evening. Mom was able to move in closer to Rio and the elm, and more children were crowding around him also, hoping a least one faery might decide to show itself at last.

An old muse named Kalliope, in the ruby-throated form of a hummingbird, drummed her wings past Morgan's ear. The girl handed to Rio the stack of remaining notes, and walked through the crowd among the elms, following the humming rhythm out around the outskirts of the grove.

Rio read more of the notes and interpreted the Faery answers as follows:

"Dear Faery,
I recently finished 2nd Grade and am wondering what direction to take my life.
Love, Shaya"

Answer: *"All roads are full of beauty and hardship. Any path you take will lead through the meadows and stones of your own heart. Happy travels!"*

"Dear Faeries,
Who do you love most - children or grownups?
Izzy"

Answer: *"Children - but everyone is a child of someone."*

"Yo,
I don't believe in you."

Answer: *"We are not here to tell you what to think, and we respect your right to believe or disbelieve as you wish. However, we should tell you that when you write a note to someone to make sure they know that you do not believe in them, it actually carries a much different meaning than you may have intended. So we thank you for your support."*

"Hi Faeries,
Can you please give me some of your powers?
From Elias"

Answer: *"You have your own powers, much more powerful and useful for you than ours would be. Discover what they are!"*

"Dear Faery,
Please help me to stop falling in love so easily!
Sincerely, Zoey"

Answer: *"Be proud of your heart that is strong and courageous enough to run free like an unbridled horse. Keep falling in love, and learning - until there be no more falling and only love remains."*

"Dear Faeries,
Do you believe in us?"

Answer: *"Yes - someone has to."*

Some of the kids had been calling out to the faeries to show themselves, but only Rio and watchful Pan would occasionally glimpse a flash of glowing color. Some of the little babies being held in the crowd could discern the glowing hues too, but to them it was just the usual glorious luster of the wide world.

The nice reporter who wore false eyelashes suddenly realized that many of the ancient stories she had read of gods and heroes and muses and dryads, were clearly about Faery beings.

Rio's schoolmate Jack, whose spirit was the laughter of the lion, asked Rio why it was that only he could speak with the faeries. Rio had assumed it had to do with his being the first one to find the Faery Door, but he asked them anyway.

They answered that even before the exile, it had always been the babes who could hear and see the shy fae best, because having newly arrived or returned to the world, their infant senses are as yet unclogged with the abstract judgments of human words. They simply see what they see, and hear what they hear. And since the veiling of Faery, the little babes have been almost the only ones to catch glimpses of the realm, but it seemed now to the fae that when Rio first opened the Faery Door, perhaps due to the intensity of all the light and song with which they had greeted him, he had stepped off of the world for a moment and then returned to find everything bright and new, and was thus like a babe, gifted again with the Faery Speech.

The children, as well as others in the crowd continued to clamor, beseeching the faeries to reveal themselves, but the Faery folk still would not dare it. Besides the vow they'd made by the moon - of their having to remain veiled until the silent heart should speak, with the sun standing still to listen, and the once deepest shadow shining like the stars - many of them just did not want to risk again the breaking of their hearts.

They were gathered in the elm tree, listening intently to the people whom they knew were imploring them to come out.

And then the voices quieted.

Like a dark star, Loki peeked out from the fork in the elm to see Morgan gently tugging Rio's hand, and motioning for him to come down from the crate, and to stand near.

She stood up on the box and looked around at the people's wondering faces, then turned to the elm to speak aloud the poem that was filling her heart, even spilling from her eyes and running down her cheeks, while she smiled shyly underneath the tears.

The starlings and finches gathered again in the boughs of the elms so that they could hear too. Hylos the sun gazed down as he drove toward the horizon. Rio and everyone in the grove listened as she sang out in her downy voice:

"Faery,
I have sought you:

Over the tide-levelled shore
on the West Wind's
wide, clear corridor;
adorned with the wave-borne
mosses crushed,
and the bleached bones of the nautilus;
Among the bending reeds
of the dark moor, brooding
under the crow's silvered wings;
In the cool wood depths of calling birds,
beneath the amber dropping boughs.

I seek for you in the harrowed fields,
in the brake shaded brooks
of unfathomable scent,
in the asphalt humbled ecologies
of vacant lot tangles
springing lush,
and along the pounded smoky roads.

All these runes long carved
into the green stone wall of my heart:
I am finding you now
I am pushing it open."

The tiny moths had taken to wing throughout the grove, like soft glitter, and the blue faery whose wings were as clear waters knew that the silent heart had spoken. She summoned a crow from its harvesting who landed by the Faery Door to lay the last wild rose of the waning year at the threshold.

"They totally heard you," Rio told Morgan, "and they really like your poem." Morgan saw the rose too, and she knew that all words spoken from the heart are magic words.

At that moment the faeries were chatting excitedly in the attic of the tree, hearing the simple rhyme of prophecy fulfilled, and the thrill of a people who more and more were reaching out to them with something much greater than fear. One of the fae, with long, fur-tufted ears hanging down beneath his acorn cap, said that he thought these people were ready to see them.

Brushing his rays over the elms, and hearing the fae discussing their possible return from exile, Hylos slowed his fall to the sea. Harvest workers along the coast began to remark to one another that this seemed to be a long day.

The guards were still watching over the tree but had taken down the barricade, and some people were gazing wide-eyed into the doorway, seeing a soft glow and hearing what sounded to them like a soft chattering of starlings and other things. Two of Rio's friends, Everett and Bella, both climbed up into the branches, thinking they might hear better from there. They had not met before, but Bella made friends by showing Everett her loose tooth. Trying to hold them as they crawled around in her almost bare limbs, the tree rocked with gladness.

The blue faery agreed with what the tuft-eared one had spoken, saying that these people actually did seem to have shaken off the dark shroud. The one with wings of starry midnight pointed out that the sun was now standing still over the horizon, which had been the almost unbelievable second sign, and just knowing this must be the day, he asked the blue faery, with the impatience of a long held dream being within reach, were they going to show themselves or not.

The blue faery whose wings were clear waters began to urge patience, reminding the others of the third sign of the prophecy - that the deepest shadow would glow like a troop of stars...

and then suddenly she realized that the deep shadow was their own; that their fear of having their hearts broken again... had long been eclipsing the most glorious flames of the hearth where their desires ever brightly burned.

As the other faeries watched, she told them this in a dance of the blooming sage, her clear wings beating gently, her heart glowing, her hands of light unmasking her eyes of light, her deep blue enhanced by each of her blue tears. Then all the faeries began to glow in such a brilliant symphony of color that no shadow could have remained among them.

And turning to him of the starry night's hues, the blue faery pronounced the one human word they knew - one of the most beautiful words of all: *"Yes."*

Mingling their bright colors, they poured joyously out of the doorway to invite the people to come out and play too...

Most of the people saw a glow of starlight amongst the flaring rays of the halted sun. They heard a vibration in the wind and the laughter of birds familiar and strange. Rio and Pan and some of the little babies in the crowd saw the vivid flames of color flying about and heard the Faery song they were singing:

> *"Awake.*
> *For the rhythm has broken;*
> *And the muted torch handed down*
> *through the ages*
> *Is ablaze once again, burning bright*
> *To light the path we have but dreamed.*
>
> *Awaken all,*
> *For the dark age is reborn as dawn;*
> *And tyranny lies hushed and fallen;*
> *And the shattered songs the prophets cried*
> *are woven into harmony anew -*
> *arise!"*

They all watched and listened amazed, while the trees, the ground, the grass, the sky, all began to blend into light. It was a light more primal and pure than the sun's or the other stars'; a light they felt with every ray of their being, rather than merely saw.

All were enraptured. The faeries sang, and the words were of sunfire and evergreen and clear eyed gulls gliding seaward over the paths of wind, but the people were beginning to hear them like Rio could:

> *"Long we stood, with our backs to the sun,*
> *Beholding naught, but our own shadows*
> *But I have turned.*
> *And in the morning I saw our spirits*
> *Mounting to the sky on roans of flame;*
> *And in the noontide I beheld*
> > *our golden nimbus*
> *Surveying all of creation;*
> *In the evening I saw our spirits*
> *Dancing out over the horizon*
> *Setting the West afire."*

The molten sun lingered over the horizon, but no shadows could be cast in the resplendent grove. The faeries sang the final verse, and the words were as subtle as tones of light, but all there could hear:

> *"And now you turn*
> *And lo, I see our angels high*
> *Summoning the purple night*
> *Tracking stars across the sky;*
> *And as you look... on toward a molten deity*
> *Lo, our spirits dawn and rise -*
> *I can gaze into your holy eyes*
> *And stare into infinity."*

No field, no earth, no space, no eyes, no tears... The doors of their senses clean and wide, all the people saw one another as they truly are - each one a boundless sea, and all worlds lying as pebbled jewels on the shores of their possibilities.

The light they saw and felt was their own.

And as they stepped back into the little world they had just left, to drift further down its stream of time and play a while longer, the people saw the Faery glows, and they could not tell whether those hues were grand or small or beyond the measure of the world. As Earth and sky appeared, they all heard the Faery voices speak as clear as the wind and the waning moon, *"Being awake means being aware of the dream and of the dreaming."*

The grove breathed peacefully as burnished shadows scattered the fragrant gold. All was bright and new, and they looked with eyes of wonder on this firefly lit universe which is a great pulsing heart we all share.

The black eyes of the downy birds glimmered with sky and praise. Rio, in the grove with Morgan, Omar, Claire, his Mom, and all the other people (Pan and the Lost Children, the police guard, Omar's moms, Harper, Sofia, the green eyed lady, the tractor driver, the nice reporter, the park workers, Diana who was sounding long tones on her djembe, the rest of his young friends, and everyone else who came to see the faeries) was very much at home among them. Hands found other hands with no need to explain anything, and the people stood together, aware of the dreaming and the dream.

The Faery lights gently swarmed around and above the brawny elms, receiving the gratitude of all, and they turned their song skyward to greet the waking stars.

Hylos and the Sea Faeries

XXIV. Dreams

Rio moved through a crowd of colors, and over near the elm to give her too his thanks. Peering into the little doorway once more, he saw another note which he was sure had not been there before the faeries came out. It was a little poem, and the hand seemed familiar:

> "I've soared above the moon-swayed depths;
> I've sailed over the sea.
> I've crossed the rolling waters
> For I left my heart with thee.
>
> I need no other compass,
> And I need no map, nor charts;
> Though I wander, you I'll always find -
> For home is where the heart is."

Rio read the stanzas and then looked over and saw his dad standing there with wonder in his eyes, seeing his son as if for the first time. His aura seemed to rise and fall like the blue swells, and dancing 'round his jacket collar were two sea green faeries murmuring like the deep waters, trying to call him back to the sea who loved him. He looked like an older, more weathered version of the boy, but having grown so accustomed to the green swells and the vast expanse, the selkies' deep eyes, and the tragic cries of the gulls, he felt somewhat out of place on land.

Having at long last sailed back into the harbor at Fort Mason as the fog was lifting a couple of hours earlier, he secured the Golden Bough to the guest dock, washed up, and then walked over to Lombard Street to catch a bus to Rio's house; but there at the bus stop he found one of the posters the kids had placed, which told him where Rio was at that moment. He hailed a taxi and got a ride to the park, and then walked in to the grove which was dazzling with the dark fires of the setting sun, and crowded with people who were holding hands, gazing skyward.

He didn't see Rio among the people at first, but he did spot what he knew must be the magic door that the poster had mentioned, in the elm with her bare limbs flocked with feathered song, her trunk now robed in scarves of silk and wool, and a leaning sign which said, "Faery, We Love You!". Walking over, and kneeling next to it, he left inside the door the poem he had written at sea, then stood shyly back against another tree and watched to see if his son would come and find his little note.

When Rio appeared and began to read his song, Dad stood in rapt amazement. And when the boy turned around and saw him, there were depths of dark seas and skies swarming with winds both fair and foul, finally traversed in the first words he spoke to his son: *"I missed you."*

The two sea fae were surprised to notice that the boy could see them. Rio could tell that his dad wasn't aware of the faeries; Dad could hear their alluring echoes, but thought it was just the sway of the blue tide in his veins.

"You've missed more than that, Man," Rio told him.

And Dad, who had sailed through abyss and storm, and earned the respect admiration of the Sea Witch, now felt afraid.

But this old man was something of a poet too, and the images of his few words did not quickly pass away; and as Rio looked into their echoes, he saw scenes of peril and steadfast courage: of high-crested storms and blind furies and torn sails, cross-currents and treacherously fallen winds, of mending sail and black fog; of speared fish and of gathering dew with tarp and pail; of a dream-wrought albatross whose looming silhouette had called down in a strange tongue, *"If there is no wind, row"*; of Dad fashioning oars with spear and fishing rod and hatch covers, and plowing through cross-currents for days and nights; of a great eye emerging from the void, and Dad casting out a slack anchor line before passing out on the deck and dreaming of being pulled by the whale who had swallowed many a straying soul; of wind and stars, and hoisting sail again; of a fire-spitting tempest who hurled the little vessel into her howling typhoon and slapped her down into the fierce chaos, Dad defiantly gripping the net he'd lashed over the cockpit and staring up through the monstrous pummelling and into the flashing black eyes of the torrent, and seeing her - and she was beautiful in her glorious rage - and calling into the hurricane, into the great universe, *"I believe in nothing but miracles!"*; of the fair dawn and a grey gull who brought him the leaf of an elm tree; of Tamalpais on her throne, rising out of the fog like an island in the sky, and Dad whispering in awe, *"Land Ho..."*; of other sails appearing on the horizons, and the Golden Gate opening in welcome, into the City where Dad had left his heart.

And Rio smiled and told his Dad, "But I'll fill you in if you'll teach me how to sail."
Dad laughed as Rio ran into his arms, and he said, "Sure, but before venturing out again, I'd better take a course in navigation!" His heart was swelling. "Actually... we could learn together!"

"So are you going to stay?" asked Mom, hoping her compassion would win over her wrath. Although their marriage had not worked out, and her old friend had lost his way, she still cared about him. "Yes," Dad said. They stood looking at each other.

Loki the dark faery laughed. These humans were hilarious.

Rio stepped away to let Mom and Dad make friends again, and his brown eyes brightly shone as he saw that peace is indeed dazzling and jubilant.

He brushed his admiration over the elm, who smiled softly with the light she had gathered during the year to last her through the slumbering Winter. He closed the Faery Door, knowing the way would stay open.

The blue faery appeared near Rio's left cheek like a warm kiss of Autumn sky. They gazed on one another in kinship, their songs to stay intertwined, and then she was up in the swirling glow of her luminous fellows.

Rio's dark eyes reflected the sky of setting sunfire, waking stars, and faeries, and he smiled as he saw that there was still and ever so much more to the world to see, so long as he kept looking. The two sea fae were now whispering in his ears.

Flames waving like purple petals, Hylos plunged his fiery chariot into the sea with a brilliant flash of deep green. And yes, just about everyone noticed.

The Blue faery whose wings were like clear water hovered above the elm, surveying the dusky grove while the sparrows began to huddle beneath the warm robes of spruce, and the willows whispered of waking dreams. The two faeries sometime known as Chamas of the Deer, and Mandwan the Burning Bush came near her. They had a couple of questions for their Blue faery.

Chamas the deer faery asked her if the people were going to break their hearts again. The Blue faery looked out over the West where the last flowers of flame were falling. And she answered that a heart will only break if it's closed too tightly around one sweet dream, and that if it does break, it should just stay broken open to embrace the whole world, and to receive its gift of light.

And Mandwan, the moth winged, Autumn leaf of the

sunset's hues asked the Blue Faery - who had once been a Valkyrie, and had also sometime been known as Aethas of the Birds - whether the world was now healed. And she answered that they had only just begun, but her indigo heart burned with the cheer of the waking stars bursting through the dusk, for she knew they would continue to work this miracle until it was accomplished, that the great song will not end until it may end well, and she gave praise to the source of her magic, with gratitude that reached beyond the farthest spheres and stars, all swaying within her sea.

The little moths felt the dusk under their wings as the tide turned toward the crescent moon and followed her blushing silver path.

A sleeping baby dreamed of the pebbled jewels on her infinite shores.

One green parrot who had ventured far from home, finally reached the land of warm rains and met her vivid green kin of the ancestral flock. And although her speech was full of Sparrow and Pigeon, they welcomed her into their fold and smoothed her travel worn plumes.

And she was grateful, but she also knew that the North Wind would soon carry down - across the plowed coastal fields rich with the silver seas, through the stony mountains ever flowered in towering pine, and over the red deserts of unwavering faith - a faint scent of the tides of fog and grey whale oceans; and then her deepest wish would be to return home in the Spring and watch the others' eyes as she spoke of her adventures. She was a spirit of Faery, as are all beings once they're awake and dreaming.

And the galaxies spun their braids of burning suns, whirling in rhythm with all things - every atom, burning leaf, and planet of this wild, savage dance; this grand, sacred, beating drum and dreaming heart of divine desolation.

And the gathering of people listened to the wordless Faery song in the twilit grove while the lights of the city burned into the night, ever searching for her soul - which never was lost.

It was an evening no more miraculous than any other.

*   *   *   *
   *   *   *

Glossary

; - a semicolon. which is used to indicate a pause that is greater than a comma, but not so final as a period.

- - a dash, usually followed by some extra information about a being or thing just mentioned.

Absolve - to find innocent; to clear away an accusation of wrongdoing.

Academy of Sciences - a museum of natural history, first built in 1874 by the Academy (a group of scientists and scholars) which was founded in 1853 .

Aljanna - the word for "faery" in the Hausa language spoken around the region of Chad in North Africa.

Angler's Lodge - built in 1938, the home of the Angling and Casting Club.

Anglo-Saxon - a term referring to the language and people who settled in Britain after the retreat of the Romans from the land, who dominated the country which came to be known by the name of the chief tribe: Angle-land (England).

Arcadia - the pastoral, mountainous country of Southern Greece; also, any such area of similar climate and landscape.

Ardent - passionate devotion or adoration.

Ash (Fraxinus uhdei) - a large, stout, deciduous tree with elongated leaves and pale, somewhat smooth bark.

Audacity - boldness, based to some degree on ignorance.

Aura - the field of spiritual energy surrounding a living being.

Aurora - Roman name for the goddess of the dawn.

Aye - yes, certainly.

Banshee - a spirit of eternal grief; the wailing woman.

Barf - slang term for vomit, as verb and noun.

Bath - a town in Southwest England, known for the reservoirs and pools built there by the Romans in the 1st century.

Beech (Fagus sylvatica) - stout, brazen tree, with fine, heart shaped leaves and which produces small nuts.

Blue Heron (Ardia herodias) - a large, long necked, long legged, and long beaked wading bird.

Bole - the trunk of a tree.

Botanical Gardens - located in Golden Gate Park, a 55 acre living showcase of 8000 species of plants.

Bough - a branch of a tree.

Brake - ferns; a thicket of ferns.

Broadcast - to widely publish by radio or other electronic means.

Bum - the rear end.

Caesar, Julius Gaius - (100BC - 44BC) Roman politician and general, who conquered Gaul, invaded Britain, and was later instrumental in overthrowing the republic, which led to the establishment of the Roman Empire. In his youth, he was kidnapped by pirates who held him for ransom, which Caesar demanded should be a large one. He also promised them he would kill them all, and after his ransomed release, he raised a fleet and did that.

Canada Goose (Branta canadensis) - a large, water loving bird with a brownish body and whitish underbelly, black head and long neck, with white patch under and around the jaws.

Canterbury Tales - written by Geoffrey Chaucer in the 14th century, the Tales of Caunterbury is a diverse collection of stories presented in the fictional format of a storytelling contest among a group of pilgrims on a journey from London to the tomb of Saint Thomas a' Becket (1118 - 1170), who had been Archbishop of the supreme church in England at Canterbury, and was buried there after being murdered for taking a stand against the king for the rights of the church against government infringement.

Celestial - of the heavens.

Cellular - (biology) made up of living cells.

Century - a span of a hundred years, and counted by some calendars, in order from around the time of Jesus of Nazareth. Thus, the 1st century refers to the period between year 1 and year 100, inclusively; the 12th century refers to the period between the year 1101 and 1200.

Ceres - a small planet which orbits 'round the sun within the asteroid belt that is between the orbits of Mars and Jupiter.

Chaos - the formless void from which as some say, the earth and heavens emerged.

Chaucer, Geoffrey - (1343 - 1400) English poet, philosopher, and scientist. His written works established his dialect of Middle English as the dominant literary language of the land.

Chestnut (Aesulus hippocastanum) - a deciduous, digitate leaved, soft timbered tree producing spiky balls in which the seeds may be found.

Chile - a long, narrow country lying along the western coast of South America.

Chronicle - an account of an event or series of events across a certain span of time.

Clover (Trifolium repens) - a low growing, three leafed little herb, called the "*seamrog*" in Ireland.

Cockpit - a recessed area in the deck of a vessel, where the steering wheel or tiller is located.

Conjure - to produce by sorcery.

Conservatory of Flowers - a huge greenhouse where grow many tropical flowers and exotic species of plant, compartmented by climate.

Cosmic - having to do with the Cosmos, that is, the universe.

Coyote - a mischievous god who, according to some Native American legends, was engaged in a prank when he created the land so as to have a place to beach his canoe.

Creation - (capitalized) the whole world and everything in it.

Crimson - a deep, darkish red.

Cromlech - a circle of upright stones used in astronomical ceremony.

Croon - soft singing; murmuring song.

Cypress (Cupressus macrocarpa) - a tall growing, broad limbed conifer tree of the coasts, with short, fleshy bunches of needles.

Daisy - a flower with a round center and ray-like petals surrounding; originally called "Day's eye".

Dandelion - a small plant with round, many petaled blooms and seeds which sail on the wind, named "Dent de lion" (French - "Tooth of Lion") for its leaves which resemble a set of fangs.

Deciduous - describing those trees which annually drop their leaves.

De Young Museum - the fine arts museum in Golden Gate Park of San Francisco, and a cultural center of the City, first opened in 1895.

Diana's Mirror - a small circular body of water

situated in the throat of a dormant volcano near the town of Nemi in South Central Italy; named for the Roman goddess of the hunt.

Dire - full of danger or threat.

Djembe - an African drum with a wide head and upper trunk, set upon a narrower, cylindrical base.

Djinn - genies; the faery population of Arabia and Persia.

Douse - to drench with water.

Drake, Sir Francis - (1540 - 1596) English knight, sea captain, and pirate, who raided Spanish dominions in the Americas and looted Spanish ships underway. During one expedition in which he wished to avoid sailing back around Cape Horn where the Spanish were, he made repairs on his ship, the Golden Hinde, in what is now Drake's Bay near Point Reyes - north of San Francisco - then struck out westward across the Pacific, and made the second circumnavigation of the world. His leadership helped defeat the Spanish Armada, enabling England to become a world power.

Drone - unmanned aircraft; flying robot.

Dream Catcher - a Native American charm used to ward off bad dreams, usually composed of a small hoop of willow, webbed with string or sinew, and given to children to keep through the night.

Dryad - a tree nymph, particularly of the oak.

Duelist - one of a pair who will fight each other, usually over a matter of pride or honor.

Eaves - the part of the roof which juts out and overhangs the exterior walls of a building.

Elm - a family of deciduous, hardwood trees, commonly featuring asymmetrical, heart shaped leaves with serrated edges.

Ere - before; sooner than.

Esoteric - that which would be understood by few; specialized knowledge.

Ethereal - like the Ether (the region of space beyond the Earth's atmosphere); the heavens.

Eucalyptus - a type of fast growing, flowering tree native to Australia, introduced into California for lumber, but found to split too easily.

Eurhythmic - a choreographed interpretation of a piece of music; a freeform dance.

Eurynome - according to one of the earliest creation stories of ancient Greece, "the goddess of all things".

Fae - a plural form of the word "faery".

Faery - (capitalized) the race and realm of all the faeries and their magical kind.

Farallon - the small, rocky islands lying about 20 miles off the coast of San Francisco; Spanish word for "sea cliff".

Fata - the Italian word for "faery".

Faux-hawk - a haircut similar to a Mohawk (with a stripe of longer hair over the top of the head from front to back) but not completely shaved on the sides.

Finch - a small, somewhat colorful seed-eating bird.

Fleet - nimble; swift; a group of ships.

Flood - the time of the high tide; the condition of it being high and full.

Flyrod - a type of fishing pole used in fly fishing.

Fold - the members of a church or the sheep belonging to the same flock.

Folly - mistakes; clumsiness; foolishness.

Fort Mason - former military post on the shore of the Golden Gate. Now a national landmark, marina, and recreational area.

Francis - (1181 - 1226) nicknamed "Francesco" (little Frenchman) by his father because of his French mother's influence who taught him to speak and dress in French style, Francis was a merry youth of an affluent Italian family. Returning from a war, disillusioned and ill, he cast off wealth and fear and any other encumbrances to living simply and happily and seeing more clearly the miraculous glory of God's world. He called all things his brothers and sisters - the wind and sun, and even the ailments that accompanied his later years. A religious order was founded among his followers (the "Franciscans") which was sanctified by the Pope and which, hundreds of years later, established the missions along the California coast, naming the settlement on the end of the peaceful peninsula after their founder who had been sainted - "San Francisco".

Fugue - a style of musical composition in which several distinct melodies are woven 'round a central theme.

Gadget - a mechanical device or machine of some nonspecific or unknown use.

Gnash - to clench and bare one's teeth.

Gnome - small, intelligent, human-like creature, usually dwelling underground and known for being skilled in arts and crafts.

Golden Bough - the mistletoe (Viscum album) referred to in the ancient Roman writer Virgil's Aeneid, in which the main character Aeneas, needing to travel to the underworld to consult a seer there, first had to find a sprig of the golden bough to take with him so that he would also be able to leave.

Golden Gate - the entrance way from the Pacific Ocean into the San Francisco Bay.

Golden Hinde - the ship of Sir Francis Drake, who sailed her around the world under another name, but then re-christened her.

Great Highway - the road running along the beach on the ocean side of the San Francisco peninsula.

Gryffin - a beast with the head and wings of an eagle and the body of a lion.

Hada - the Spanish word for "faery".

Hand - a given style or manner of handwriting.

Harbinger - one who announces an arrival.

Harrow - to turn over the soil, breaking up the clods and making ready for plowing.

Harvest - the time of the gathering of crops or ripened fruits, often celebrated by festivals such as Halloween, Samhain, and Dia de Los Muertos.

Hawthorn - a type of tree with finely lobed leaves and red berries.

Hearken - to listen.

Hearth - the place in the house for the fire.

Henchmen - a kind of servant who may act as a body guard or attack force.

Herald - an announcer; town crier.

Hickory - a type of deciduous hardwood tree with compound leaves and large nuts.

Highlander - a native or inhabitant of the mountains in the North and West of Scotland.

Hippies - a name given to the young American people who during the 1960s, primarily in protest to what they saw as another pointless war, decided to drop out of society and pursue art, enlightenment, and social experiment.

Holly - (Ilex aquifolium) an evergreen shrub with shiny, dark green, prickly leaves and red berries.

Hordes - armies; mobs.

Jay - (Cyanocitta stelleri) the smallest member of the crow family, the jays around Golden Gate Park are dark headed, blue bottomed, and crested. Their calls are harsh yells, and they can imitate the shrieks of hawks too, to scare other birds away from an area.

Jig - a groovy Irish dancing tune.

Joan of Arc - (Jeanne d'Arc, 1412 - 1431) a French peasant girl who heard the voices of Saints Michael, Catherine, and Margaret telling her to crown the rightful Charles VII king of France, and recover the nation from English control. Charles sent her into battle with his army and the English were defeated and Charles was crowned. Joan's mission was over then and she wanted to go back home to her farm, but Charles kept her on as a political asset. She was subsequently betrayed, imprisoned by the English, tried as a witch and burned at the stake. Many years later, the charges were seen as being false, and Joan was recognized as a saint by the Church.

Juan Fernandez Islands - an archipelago (string of islands) situated in the Pacific Ocean a few hundred miles off the coast of Chile in South America. They are known for being the place where the sailor Alexander Selkirk had been marooned for four years during the late 18th century, inspiring the story of Robinson Crusoe.

Kalliope - the ancient Greek muse of epic poetry.

Kin - family; relatives.

Knoll - a small hill.

Lair - den; home.

Lavender - (Lavendula officinalis) a richly fragrant shrub producing soft, pale green, small, elongated leaves, and small purple blooms.

Legions - troops of soldiers, thousands of them.

Lenke - (Afzelia africana) a hard African wood used in shipbuilding and for making the djembe drum.

Lest - unless; in prevention of.

Lilac - (Syringa vulgaris) a shrub that blooms in clusters of light purple blooms.

Litany - a chanted prayer.

Lithe - flexible and strong.

Lo - behold; look.

Lombard - a street running from the Marina District over to the North Beach neighborhood, where it becomes "the windiest street in the world".

Lore - data and knowledge about a thing.

Lot - the chance circumstances.

Lupine - any number of flowering plants of the pea family, with elongated floral clusters - which in California may be blue, purple, or yellow - digitated leaves, and seed pods.

Mandarin Chinese - the principal language of China; the dialect used by the Chinese national government.

Memorial Grove - (National AIDS Memorial Grove) a beautiful garden of trees, shrubs, and flowers dedicated in 1991 to the many people who have died from the AIDS disease (Auto-Immune Deficiency Syndrome).

Mercury - the planet closest to the sun; the messenger of the Roman gods.

Merlin's Oak - an oak tree which stood in the town

square of Caefyrddin, Wales which was said to be the birthplace of Merlin, the wizard and advisor of King Arthur of the Britons.

Middle East - the area of the world around Persia (which is now under the flags of Iran, Iraq, Afghanistan, and a few other nations), and Arabia.

Midsomer (Midsummer) - the time around the Summer Solstice.

Milky Way - the galaxy of which our sun and its solar system are but an extremely rural suburb among one of its sparse outer rings.

Minion - a helper; a favorite or friend.

Mirth - laughter and cheer.

Mission Dolores - founded in 1776 by the Franciscan Order who were building missions along the coast, the encampment was named San Francisco after their founder, but the chapel was named "Nuestra Senora de los Dolores" (Our Lady of Sorrows) which refers to Mary and some of the things she had to endure as the mother of Jesus, the messiah.

Mistletoe - (Viscum album) a parasitic plant that grows on other trees, piercing their bark with its roots, and remaining green or gold even after the host tree has dropped its leaves for the Winter season.

Mockingbird - (Mimus polyglottos) a grey, black, and white bird whose song is composed to some degree of the echoed calls of other birds as well as of other surrounding sounds.

Monastery - the residence of an order of monks (religious hermits and scholars).

Moor - open land where sweep the wild winds, and so only the hardiest grasses and shrubs will thrive.

Mote - speck of dust.

Mourning Dove - (Zenaida macroura) a grey, brown, and softly pink seed-eating dove whose song sounds like soft weeping.

Mozart, Wolfgang Gottlieb - (1756 - 1791) brilliant Austrian composer of opera and chamber music which are often bright simplicities woven out of complex harmonies and movements.

Muse - those spirits who inspire the poets and composers.

Nana - a name which many babies come up with on their own for their grandmother (perhaps left over from the Faery speech).

Naught - nothing.

Nautilus - (Nautilus bauensis) a swimming shellfish related to the octopus; the name of the first submarine invented by Robert Fulton, and the name of the vessel featured in Twenty Thousand Leagues Under the Sea, by Jules Verne.

Neptune - the Roman god of the sea; another name for Poseidon.

Network - a group of news stations who share the same stories and gossip.

Nimbus - a halo; a hazy ring seen 'round the moon.

Norman French - the language spoken by the Normans who during the Middle Ages had come from the North to settle in France, and then conquered England where their language slowly mixed with the Old English spoken by the Anglo-Saxons.

Nymph - a spirit, often that of a tree or flower or river or something; a faery.

Oberon - in Shakespeare's Midsomer Nights Dreame, the king of the faeries.

Ohlone - the tribes of people who for thousands of years before the Europeans arrived, had lived around the San Francisco Bay region, hunting and gathering, and generally at peace with one another.

Oppositional Defiance Disorder - a "mental illness" often characterized by an unwillingness to receive psychiatric treatment. Usual symptoms include: not wishing to have high voltage electrodes attached to one's head; not wishing to ingest toxic, mind-altering drugs; not desiring to be locked up in a cell without having committed an actual crime; and the protesting of these things.

Orion - son of Poseidon and the queen of the Amazons, Orion lived in exile as a lone hunter until he was befriended by Artemis, the goddess of the moon who was then tricked into killing him by her brother Apollo; a constellation most prevalent in the Winter months.

Painted Lady (Cynthia anabella) - a colorful species of butterfly which can periodically be seen in migration through California, and sometimes used in funerals and weddings, being released at a given point.

Pan - the ancient Greek god of the wild and of shepherds and flocks and rustic music. The word "panic" is derived from his name due to the silliness of people being frightened upon beholding him.

Peerless - having no equal.

Phoenix - the immortal and gloriously plumed bird of legend who is consumed in its own flame at the end of a lifetime, but then rises from the ashes to live for another span.

Pioneer Cabin - an old log house which was

originally built during the pioneer days, up near the Oregon border where it stood before being taken down and reassembled in Golden Gate Park.

Pixie - a colorful faery.

Point Reyes - a cape jutting out from the California Coast north of San Francisco Bay.

Poison Oak (Toxicodendron diversilobum) - a bush with leaves similar in shape to an oak, but which always grow in sets of three. The leaves and stems carry an oily sap that can cause an itchy allergic rash in some people. Deer love to eat the tender leaves.

Poseidon - the ancient Greek god of the sea.

Press - the people and operations involved with a printing press, now chiefly used to refer to news reporters.

Pride - the collective term for lions, and now gryffins too.

Prologue - an introduction or preliminary attachment to a piece of literature; the foreword.

Puck - in Shakespear's Midsummer Night's Dream, the jester and assistant to Oberon, King of the Faeries.

Quarry - prey; someone or something being pursued.

Redwood - common name for the sequoia tree, which is an evergreen conifer, some of which are among the tallest and oldest living things on Earth.

Resplendent - filled with brilliant luster.

Roan - a reddish-brown horse speckled with grey or white.

Rouse - to waken; to stir.

Rune - ancient form of writing, the individual letters representing both phonetic sounds as well as symbolic depictions.

Rushes - the pithy grasses growing in or near creeks

and other wetlands.

Russet - reddish brown.

Sage (Salvia officinalis) - an aromatic herb which grows as a shrub with soft, pale green, elongated leaves.

Saint Elmo's Fire - an electrical glow sometimes seen around upright objects such as trees or masts during a thunderstorm. Named after Erasmus of Formia, the patron saint of Sailors.

Sapphire - a translucent, blue gem.

Saroyan, William - (1908 - 1981) brilliant American author and playwright who shows magic in simple settings and everyday events.

Schooner - sailing vessel of two or more masts, the foremost being shorter than those aft (behind).

Score - an amount of twenty.

Selkie - a seal whose soul had sometime been human too.

Sentience - awareness; having the ability to think and feel and to know that one is thinking and feeling.

Seven Woods - (In the Seven Woods) Yeats' collection of poetry composed while out walking in the seven woods around his home, published in 1903

Shakespear, William - (1564 - 1616) ("the Bard") brilliant English poet and playwright, whose lines sometimes capture depths and subtleties of the human soul not described anywhere else.

Shakespeare Garden - a hedged acre within the park, dedicated to the Bard and featuring a wall of bronze plaques embossed with quotes from the plays of every mention of herb and flower.

Shanti - a translation of the Sanskrit (language used in ancient India) word for "peace" and "serenity".

Sharon Field (or Meadow) - a roughly five acre field situated near Sharon Art Studio and the Koret Playground and Carousel, good for soccer practices, and overlooked by Hippie Hill - where many a drum circle has taken place.

Sierra - the high, snowy mountains running along California's Eastern border; Spanish word for "mountain range". It's full name is the Sierra Nevada (nevada means "snowy").

Snarky - making critical jokes or remarks.

Sought - past tense form of "seek".

Spanglish - Spanish with English words and forms mixed in.

Sparrow - small, often brownish, seed eating birds.

Sprite - a magical spirit.

Spruce - a family of coniferous, evergreen trees, many of which feature short, even needle bunches.

Stanzas - in poetry, the paragraphs or sections of verse.

Starling (Sturnus Vulgaris) - a blackbird like species, speckled and iridescent, possessing a wide range of song and calls, introduced into America from Europe in the 19th century by someone attempting to bring to the New World every bird species mentioned in any of Shakspeare's plays.

Stow Lake - the largest lake in Golden Gate Park, holding several islands, and on which sits a boathouse where one may rent rowboats or paddleboats by the hour.

Strings - the section of an orchestra which includes those playing instruments such as the violin and the cello.

Sundance - a dance done to celebrate the sun, or to

encourage its arrival and shine.

Sunder - to tear apart; divide; cut.

Tai chi - a Chinese martial art with roots in Buddhism and Taoism, and emphasizing not oppositional or combative moves, but rather the practice of moving with All. The term in Chinese means "boundless fist".

Tea Tree (Leptospermum ericoides) - a shrub with small elongated leaves, elaborately twisted trunks, hard wood, and dark, sometimes raggedy bark.

Tempest - a violent storm.

Thermos - brand name for a kind of insulated bottle for carrying liquids that one wishes to stay cool or warm.

Thicket - a clump of trees or high shrubs; a dense grove.

Thistle (Asteraceae carduus) - a spiky leaved plant with a fuzzy purple flower.

Thrush - a family of birds which include robins and bluebirds.

Thus - as such; therefore.

Tidings - news; announcements.

Tinker Bell - a faery from the works of J.M. Barrie, whose inspiration upon the imaginations and the dreams of children and adults is beyond measure.

Tir Na Nog - (Irish) "Land of the Young"; the Faery land of everlasting youth.

Titan - in ancient Greek legend, of the gods who were the predecessors to the later Olympian gods.

Tongues (Speaking in) - the inspired rambling chant sometimes heard in Christian or other religious ceremony, sometimes said to be the language of the angels.

Tresses - lengths of one's hair.

Try - to put on trial; to judge.

Tunder - the Hungarian word for "faery".

Twilight - the time just before night, when all earthbound shapes appear as dark silhouettes.

Twin Peaks - the two highest peaks in San Francisco, standing side by side and of about equal elevation and shape.

Twylyth Teg - Welsh term for "faery", meaning one of the "fair family".

Unwieldy - hard to carry; heavy.

Valkyrie - one of those spirits who in the Norse tales, would usher the valiant warriors slain in battle, to the realm of Valhalla where they may feast and fight merrily until Ragnarok - the twilight of the gods and the final battle in which all will be destroyed.

Venus - second stone from the sun; the evening star.

Vila - a word for "faery" from the Croatian language of Eastern Europe.

Victorian - a style of house utilizing ornate structure and trim, built during the reign of Queen Victoria of Great Britain (1837 - 1901). During that time, they were not called Victorian, but were called "Queen Anne" style - after an earlier monarch who reigned from 1702 - 1714.

Virga - curtains of rain hanging from clouds and not yet fallen far or near the ground.

Waning - getting smaller; coming to an end.

Wayfarer - wanderer; traveller.

West Wind - the wind which comes from the West.

Whence - from where; from which place.

Wild Swans - (The Wild Swans at Coole) the title of a collection of poetry by Yeats, published in 1917.

Coole is a thousand acre park in County Galway, Ireland.

Willow - family of trees which grow in cool climates and moist soils, usually featuring leaves that are much longer than wide.

Wind (The) - gas; flatulence.

Wrought - fashioned by art and skill; hand made.

Yarrow (Achillea millefolium) - an herb with feathery leaves, flowering at the top of a long stalk in a plane of tiny, usually white blooms.

Yeats, Willam Butler - (1863 - 1939) Irish playwright, poet, statesman, and cultural beacon.

Yggdrasil - the ancient ash tree of Norse legend, said to be supporting the earth and heavens and netherworlds.

Yule - the Winter solstice festival to celebrate the rebirth of the sun, when the days have ceased to shorten and are beginning to lengthen again.

About the Author:

T. Powell is a poet, carpenter, rare book dealer, and dad. He lives aboard his sailing vessel, the Shanti. You may find out more about his and Rio's work with the Faery folk at:

www.faerydoor.net